# This Is **PUSH**

# GO THERE.
## OTHER TITLES AVAILABLE FROM **PUSH**

# This Is **PUSH**

### *An Anthology of New Writing by*

Coe Booth

Kevin Brooks

Eireann Corrigan

Eddie de Oliveira

Tanuja Desai Hidier

Brian James

Kristen Kemp

Christopher Krovatin

Patricia McCormick

Billy Merrell

Matthue Roth

Samantha Schutz

Kevin Waltman

Chris Wooding

Markus Zusak

*Edited by David Levithan*

**SCHOLASTIC INC.**

NEW YORK   TORONTO   LONDON   AUCKLAND   SYDNEY

MEXICO CITY   NEW DELHI   HONG KONG   BUENOS AIRES

ISBN-13: 978-0-439-89028-1
ISBN-10: 0-439-89028-4

12 11 10 9 8 7 6 5 4 3 2 1                     7 8 9 10 11 12/0

Printed in the U.S.A.                                        40
First printing, February 2007

# This Is PUSH

*Thanks, as always, to the entire PUSH team. The authors. The readers. Erin Downing, Anica Rissi, Joshua Glazer, and Ranya Fattouh from the editorial team. Steve Scott and the art department. Bonnie Cutler and the production department. The sales, marketing, publicity, manufacturing, legal, and other departments at Scholastic. All of our interns.*

*Everyone who's been there from the start – you know who you are. And everyone who'll be there for the future – you know who you'll be.*

*— DL*

# THE LOST CHAPTER

## by Eireann Corrigan

His name wasn't Ben; it was Jim. I changed it for the book and have felt guilty for that since. But back then I felt guilty for other reasons — the brief mentions of him, the fact that I wrote a whole book for a whole other boy. In that book, he was only a side story. But his name was Jim, and he loved to snowboard and was so skinny that he was always cold and wore long johns under his clothes in the winter.

He wrote poetry and that's how we met. I was in high school, had just been released from the hospital and wore that like some kind of sophistication. I wore heels all the time and mentioned my "recovery" often in front of strangers. I still threw up, still lived for days on sugar-free Jell-O and diet soda. I still fit in clothes from the sixth grade. And every Thursday I dragged my friends to the open mic at this place called Café News in New Brunswick, New Jersey. And read poems about all that crap. Recovery, my ass.

He and his friends always sat at the corner wooden table with the chessboard painted on the top, and he was the only one whose poems didn't suck. He spoke slowly like he was smoking a cigarette but exhaling words. I couldn't look at him unless he was on stage, sitting on the stool beneath the spotlight, because I felt weird staring at a table full of college guys. And then when I read, I made eye contact with anyone in the crowd except him. When he went to the counter to get coffee, I'd follow behind him, just to get to know him a little better, just to have the chance to memorize how his shoulders looked beneath his shirt.

Daniel, the kid I wrote most of my poems about, was in college and on acid and generally unavailable. And this guy had even bluer eyes and wrote poems and went to Rutgers nearby. I didn't have to wait for winter break to see him. I spent two months making sure we stood next to each other on the coffee line, spent rides home giggling to my friends because he and I had smiled at each other, or moaning because we hadn't. And then I finally wrote a poem called "in place of my phone number, for someone who won't ask for it." I stood up and read it right at him. I could hardly believe that I did it. And that something so embarrassing could actually work — that night he strolled up to me and introduced himself and told my friend Nicole that he'd drive me home that night.

My parents approved of him so intensely that they moved my curfew back an hour, even though he had hair to his shoulders and drove a red sports car and my brother said he looked like he smoked weed. Which he did. Most nights we went back to his dorm room instead of whatever movie we claimed to be seeing. His was the first body I really understood, really got to know. And I trusted him with mine in a way that had previously seemed impossible. Some anorexics get flashy with their frailness. I didn't — I wore layers and layers of clothes, and hated to be embraced. But with Jim it was different. Maybe because

2

he was so skinny — we wore the same size pants. Or maybe it was just his gentleness, his immense kindness. We'd sit in his car and he'd play a tape of Lou Reed singing, "I'll be your mirror." He brushed my hair. When we first had sex, I didn't cry, but he did. And then he teased me for keeping on my socks the whole time.

Back then, I was obsessed with the idea of sleeping next to someone else. For me that meant true love, that meant romance. I remember thinking what a luxury it would be to sleep curled against him for a whole night, to not have to throw our clothes on and speed to my house by midnight. Sometimes we'd get back to my house early and watch TV in the darkened den just so I could doze off with my head on his chest. And Jim would ease out from under me, tuck a blanket around me, and let himself out.

On Thursdays, we sat together at the café and read maudlin poems about each other at the open mic. His poems begged me to eat and mine begged him to quit bugging me to eat. We went to vintage shops and tried on silver suits and velvet hats. My sister managed a bookstore and hired Jim, so I'd sit in one of the armchairs reading while he shelved magazines. For some reason we liked to park his little red car in church lots and fool around. He loved carrot cake and I learned to make it from scratch. We traded books and left notes for each other in their margins.

I wasn't a good girlfriend. Maybe because I spent so much time hurting myself, I developed a talent for damage. Maybe because I was still so hung up on Daniel. Because I'd missed so much while I was in the hospital for my eating disorders, maybe I felt like the world owed me something and back then Jim was

3

the main deliveryman. I ended up resenting his gentleness. When my thick acceptance envelope came from Sarah Lawrence College, he saw it as a new open mic and a life without curfews. But it looked to me like an exit strategy.

And then that June, we ran into Daniel on the street outside Café News. He was home from college and when I saw him it felt the same way it always did when I saw him — like my lungs had suddenly turned themselves inside out and pressed my heart up my throat. For a second we all stood there on the sidewalk, the three of us shifting our weight and studying the pavement. Somehow I managed to introduce them. The two of them shook hands and I wanted Daniel to suffer a little, seeing me with someone else. I hung on Jim and then spent too much time watching Daniel walk away. Jim and I sat in the car and yelled at each other until it was time to take me home. Almost a month later, we were pretty much breaking up, but we went to a party in the garden of one of Jim's professors, danced on the patio, and drank wine out of ceramic mugs. Days later I found the article in the newspaper about how Daniel had been found shot on his cellar floor. And everything else stopped mattering then.

There's a whole book about the summer I sat next to Daniel's hospital bed, watching the monitors and machines like they were some soap opera marathon. *You Remind Me of You* was so slim and narrow and we pretty much figured it couldn't hold that much recklessness, so many lousy decisions. So Jim became Ben and that story got streamlined into a sudden, unexpected, and terrible event. But the truth is more complicated than that.

That fall I read my poems at the Dodge Poetry Festival, and so the last time I saw Jim, he was standing in an audience.

Wearing a sweater I used to fall asleep against, listening to me read poems about how much I loved my brave and injured boyfriend, Daniel. Or maybe he wasn't listening. By then he was high most of the time — he'd driven me to the festival and I remember being fearful riding in the car beside him. We'd planned to camp there with friends, but when we got out to set up the tent he was too blurry and addled. The tent went up all lopsided and we didn't even hammer most of the pegs into the ground. It was late September and cold and I ended up catching a ride back up to Sarah Lawrence and not staying over. My sister called the next week and asked me to call Jim. He kept showing up to work late, he'd broken his arm somehow, had quit looking people in the eye. She thought he was depressed. Maybe I could talk him into getting some kind of help. She thought I'd want to know.

I didn't call. I didn't want to know. In those days, I counted myself as responsible for reminding one boy to stay alive, and that was Daniel. That is the cold, hard truth of what happened. I was nineteen and tired of being reliable. It was two weeks later that I stopped into my dorm room between lunch and my shift at the music library. The phone rang and it was a girl from back home, the same one who'd told me that Daniel had shot himself — that there had been no intruder, no violent drug dealer or hostage situation. She was already crying when I answered. Jim was heading home from his family's cabin in the mountains and he must have swerved. They found the car pleated against a tree on the side of the road.

He was still alive then, his family at his side. I could picture it so clearly. The bright glare and stale Tupperware smell of the hospital. Jim waking up and then the months of slow progress.

Surgeries and casts and scars that we'd rub with vitamin E until they faded into his skin. I really never expected that he wouldn't live. I called home and my parents offered to come get me, but I figured I'd take the train the next morning — Daniel had shot himself in the face and survived. It felt inconceivable that Jim wouldn't be the new miracle in town. So I sat for seven hours at the desk in the music library, checking out recordings and sets of headphones. It never felt like the last of anything. At eight o'clock, I circled around the tiny library, shutting off all the stereos. I locked up and stepped into the dark lot to walk home. Probably when I saw my parents' car parked in front of my dorm, I knew. And then I saw my dad standing at the door and knew harder.

I'd been useful at Daniel's bedside as a thing — a bribe — a girl. At Jim's funeral, I felt like one of the objects in the room that he had once held. Like his guitar, like his baseball glove. Something he had once placed his hands on and was, therefore, weirdly valuable. At the wake, there were pictures on easels throughout the room. Jim as a little kid, missing teeth and up at bat. Sitting in front of the Christmas tree with the dog in his lap. There were pictures of Jim and me at the café, of us leaning into each other at the prom. We walked through a gauntlet of pictures and I stayed shielded between my parents, behind my sister. It felt like people saw me and knew, that maybe I carried some secret disease that weakened the boys who reached out for me.

I knelt in front of him and made myself look. And he didn't look like himself at all. He looked thick and pained and it made me realize how rarely I'd ever watched him sleep — I didn't recognize him without seeing his blue eyes. It could have been

6

someone else in there. And then the next morning, when we got to the cemetery, an ambulance raced ahead of us, with the lights on and sirens shattering the quiet. All I could think was that Jim had woken up just in time. Just how I'd known it would happen. But of course that wasn't true. Jim's grandmother had suffered a heart attack. And so his mom lost her mom that day, too.

Right before I graduated high school, they sat us down and had us each write a letter to ourselves. We sealed them and the alumni office held them for the next few years, then sent them on to us in the winter of our senior year in college. Mine said, "Probably you still write poems and chase boys. I hope by now you've moved on from Jim and gotten over Daniel." It was like my stodgy little prep school had mailed me a letter bomb. And I read and reread it, repeatedly detonating.

I couldn't stop thinking about that sidewalk collision. Three weeks before Daniel in his basement and all of it that came after. There were three of us and there's no good reason why Daniel and I got the chance to grow out of how we hurt ourselves and each other. Why Jim didn't. Sometimes Daniel and I would stand in a room and it would feel like the whole rest of the world tilted. That everyone else simply slid off the planet. But then Jim actually did. We used to tell ourselves that we at least owed it to Jim to love each other hard and well, as if that could somehow make it worth the world losing him. But of course it couldn't. Not even on the planet of the most selfish. Not even on the ninth moon of the most careless. There's no way really to make the death of anyone make sense. Especially not a twenty-one-year-old. Not even as a literary device.

Jim was twenty-one when he died and it's weird to think of

him that way, as a kid, really, so much younger than I am now. Some skater punk skidding between two cars stopped in traffic. Who poured more milk in his coffee than coffee. Mornings I run along the same river that twists behind my old high school and I don't expect that he's watching over me. Hopefully he's doing better things, he's reentered the world in the way he hoped and believed. He's an owl, he's an elm. He's something as still and steady as how we knew him to be. But there are still times that I talk to the sky, and by the sky I mean Jim. Try to explain the life I have now to the same color blue that used to flash in his eyes.

They were blue like the sky at three o'clock in July and his handwriting slanted slightly to the right. Sometimes he tied a navy bandanna over his hair and he usually wore wool socks with sandals. Most of the time when he laughed, his face crinkled up silently and whether he was stirred by anger or beauty, he shook his head — like either way he was trying to see more clearly. In his poems, he favored words with one syllable and often compared ordinary things to stars. He could eat an entire box of Cinnamon Toast Crunch cereal in one sitting and knew the words to *Where the Wild Things Are* by heart. His name wasn't Ben. It was James Mitchell Anderson. And he wasn't a minor character to anyone who knew him.

# THE FIRST SIX KILLERS

### by Markus Zusak

*For Eva, my friend.*

### 53 Killers: An Introduction

My name is Henry Shipps.

I have a face like darkness. I have a smile like an uncomfortable tide.

My father is Arnold Shipps.

My mother is Zelda Shipps.

Arnold Shipps also has a darkness face, but he has a smile like a shoulder. Zelda Shipps has red hair. Her face is white and a little bit gray, like the clouds.

The truth about me is that people like to call me a freak. This is through every fault of my own, considering that I am sixteen and I like to drift. I rarely speak. My voice sounds like a crooked trolley. I am like a rainy day. I am needed but no one really wants me. Still, I smile about this fact. I find the time.

Also, I can play the flute.

I like to play it at the cemetery.

Dead people are quite kind.
But they never clap.

As to the point of these pages, I have discovered something.
    Something true.

I have discovered that there are 53 killers in all of us.
    53 killers in a human leaf.
    53 killers in you,
    and in me.

## killer #1: fear

You might think me strange for playing my flute in the cemetery, but it's not really so freakish, or perhaps sinister, as you might think.

It's Aretha who makes me do it.

Aretha's a lovely girl.

She's not so good-looking as other girls. She has a pimple or two and she has brown hair. She isn't too skinny either and she has pretty average legs.

But she can certainly be beautiful, on her day.

She's mildly popular and ignores me at school and other public places. I do not despise her or blame her for this. People think me strange, and I'd hate for her to also be considered as such, by association.

Aretha comes to the cemetery on Saturday mornings, when I work there. Mostly I dig graves, but if no people have died recently I do some gardening work. More people die than you think.

My boss, Mr. Hutchinson, is what you would call a burly man. He's always in a suit and a crooked tie. He refuses to buckle to progress; therefore I dig graves manually rather than scoop them out with machinery. Another thing about Mr. Hutchinson is that he does not necessarily like me. In fact, I'd say he tolerates me, implying consistently that I am bludging. I think this arose from the time I finished digging a grave and Aretha jumped in and I played my flute for her. He caught us.

There are many worse things to catch people doing.

Saturday is routine, like this:
My alarm clock goes off at 6 A.M.
My cornflakes are earthquakes in the still of morning.
I brush my teeth.
I go to work.

If I see on the news, like I did a few nights ago, that some deaths have occurred, I know it will be a long day.

A few nights ago, three clumsy-headed youths tried to hold up a service station and one shot the other through the chest.
The odds are that he will be buried in a grave that I have dug.
Unless they burn him.
Personally, I would like to be burned when I die.

I fear death quite heavily.
But I have felt a fear greater than death once before. It concerns my alarm clock.

It was Christmas and I wanted to get up and watch *The Little Drummer Boy* and *Frosty the Snowman* on the television, and in my excitement I woke up too early. In the orange-lit lounge room, I watched the legendary yuletide cartoons. I forgot to switch off the alarm and when it went off and I didn't hear it, Arnold Shipps went in and smashed the clock to pieces on the floor.

He then walked back to bed, just as Frosty came to life — "HAP-PY BIRTH-DAY!!!"

Next, my mother, Zelda Shipps, stormed through the lounge room, went outside, smashed the mugs my dad had bought her with her consent for Christmas, then returned and picked up a board game called *Careers*. When she re-entered the bedroom, she threw it at him.

A dry shower of fake money floated down around them.

She also threw her quite heavy jewelry box at my father's head.

The damage was not permanent.

_____ A certain fear killed me that day, but I survived.

<u>killer #2: risk</u>

When I dig a grave, I feel like I have eyes the color of dirt. I would not like someone to shovel them, though.

Sometimes I dig a grave and it's deep enough to cause me strife getting out of. (I like the word *strife*.) When this occurs, I dig a small foot hole with my fingers and then climb out of the grave, like it's a ladder. I did this on the day I met Aretha.

I was digging quite a nice grave in the general admittance area (they don't care what race or religion you are to be buried there — you just have to be a corpse), when people were gathering close by on the cusp of the Catholic section.

Hymns and crying mingled with the sound of my shovel. When I was finished, I climbed from the grave and ate an apple with my grubby hands.

The funeral was like a merry-go-round. The people circled the grave.

I ate my apple.

Many hours went by, and when I finished my last grave of the day, I noticed there was still a girl standing there. She was the one kid who refused to get off the ride.

When I was about to pack up and head home, I decided I couldn't simply leave her standing on her own.

She wore a black dress and black shoes that were too big.

The trees of the cemetery are also too big.

14

Their shade is like voices. When it's windy it's like they're clearing their throats.

You can't leave someone standing there on her own, shrouded by all those voices.

Slowly, I walked over and stood next to her.

Nerves had bent down inside me.

They then carried themselves up from my stomach, like a road train. Inside them were these things:

- a sentence or two.
- handfuls of risk.

Standing there, I reached for some risk and hesitantly offered it to the girl. I said:

"Nice day for a funeral."

I don't think this was exactly the right thing to say, because the girl only looked at me and let astonishments of tears roll down her face.

Next, she began to beat me.

She slapped my throat and slumped her fists into my ribs.

A stray palm collapsed on my nose.

Like I said, I don't think it was quite the right thing to say.

But it was a risk I'm glad I took.

We stood there, the girl and me.

We stood amongst the voice shadows, the graves and the cooling tears on her face.

The girl stared at the grave.
    I stared at her shins.

_____ Risk delivered me that day. It carried me. It killed me, making me smile.

<u>killer #3: death</u>

Death was killing Aretha.

It was her grandmother who had died, but that death was lodged in the girl's stomach as she remained, still breathing.

There was a small opening in the trees, where light streamed in like a gift. There were fists of clouds in the sky.

When Aretha stopped beating me and the blood had turned stiff on my skin, she spoke. She had a voice like miss-hit piano notes and words like stones falling into a bath.

"She'd bought a new television recently," she told me. "Did you know that?"

I replied faithfully.

"No, I didn't."

"But she didn't know how to use the remote control," she explained. "And she always sang one song."

I pulled at the blood on my lip, perhaps to let more words out. My whisper was a voice. "What was it?"

"Something about dominoes and sad eyes. She sang it in German."

"Was she German?"

"No."

We both faced the air, speaking words into it. "She knew a slaughterman who was German. He was a nice man but his trade haunted him. Even his nickname was Slaughterman, and later, just Slaughter."

Soon she continued with the story of the television. "The trouble was that she saw nothing on it, because you had to tune it in with the remote."

I pictured the old lady sitting in her lounge-room dark, watching all that snow.

When Aretha left, I was standing there, alone.

I turned and made sure to witness her calves and the backs of her legs in general. She walked with her arms folded, like she was cold.

"Good-bye," I wanted to say, but I didn't speak or mention anything.

In truth, I wanted her to thank me. I wanted her to apologize for hitting me and bloodying up my nose.

But nothing came.

I only looked down at my grave-digging shirt.

Right down the middle of it, there was a staircase of blood.

_____ I think the prospect of death made Aretha die that day, just a little, inside. Sometimes death can kill you. It leaves you standing there, still alive.

## killer #4: lust

I think I was four years old when I first felt lust.

I was in the supermarket and there was a small girl with crinkle-cut hair, a smile like a toy, and cheeks filled with artificial cherry coloring. I couldn't get her out of my mind. I tried but I constantly failed.

Recently I've stayed up late, watching a very old show called *Magnum, P.I.* The only untrue part of that last statement is that I don't actually watch it. I turn my back and think about a girl in my math class named Kristy Hawkes. She has caught me staring at her and has clearly labeled me as quite invariably unhinged. But I love to fondle her in my mind.

As Magnum discusses things with Higgins, his associate, I am in a hidden room of my mind, undressing Kristy Hawkes. She likes our bodies to touch, chest to chest.

When I imagine this, my stomach drops with great embarrassment and great thrill.

Eventually sleep falls on top of me, like alcohols.

Yes, *alcohols*, with an *s*.

And I wake up, alone, next to a snoring TV.

Another truth is that I've also had dreams of lust concerning Aretha. I like her shins and the rest of her.

In the dream, I lick her ankles and make my way up. I kiss the inner part of her thighs, and nervously, my hand sweats and creases her black funeral dress.

Her approving voice is a sponge.

It soaks me up.

Again I wake up alone.

I think I've had that dream twenty-four times now. I often have it the night before work, and when Aretha shows up at the cemetery the next day, the nervousness wets my hands.

"Hi, Aretha."
"Hi, Henry."

I know that she does not have lustful dreams concerning me. In fact, I wonder why she continues coming to see me on these Saturdays.

I will dig and then notice her face.
It climbs down.

Again, I lick her legs, in my mind.
The lust thickens.
I dig.

Later, I play my flute and Aretha smiles.
"Play the Beethoven one," she says. "I like that one."
The skin beneath my mouth is cooled by the calm, cold metal of the instrument. It's a little aggressive, this piece, but as I play and the smell of dirt and coffins is shoveled up my nose, I am still licking Aretha's inner thighs.

_____ Lust is a gun. Glorious, hourly bullets.

<u>killer #5: love</u>

Should I tell you about the day I fell in love with Aretha? I think I had better.

Despite having quite a large number of lustful dreams about her (I count twenty-four as quite a few), I have also been in love with her for a fair while now. It occurred originally because of orange peels and roadkill.

It had been a demanding, taxing day at the cemetery. I had dug several graves and barely had time to play the flute. Aretha was reading out loud from a book called *Welcome to the Cheap Seats* by someone called Eva Whatevs. It was mainly a book of poems and musings, and what one critic described as "quite boss pictures."

As Aretha read, my fingers bled.

Also I remember her voice as being different then.
    I was not in love with her.

Later, though, her voice gave me a cracked mouth and a dry riverbed throat.

We were walking home when Aretha stopped.
    I remember because I was examining the blood and dirt that had lined in the cracks of my fingers. I hadn't washed my hands at the cemetery shed. I didn't want my skin to burn just then.

21

The road we walked on was highway and Aretha's feet clenched shut.

She'd been eating an orange.

A trail of peels swerved behind us.

Once she had stopped, I noticed she was watching something up ahead. There was a dead fox on the side of the road. Its mouth was open, a tortured yawn. It was bored of being dead.

It's very clear, this memory.

The blood of it.

The dry, red dirt under my fingernails.

Aretha stood, like that day on the cusp of the Catholic section. She was silent for quite a while, as traffic lingered past. She dropped the orange. It clapped to the ground, small and white.

"I just —"

They were the only words she permitted herself to say as a tear sank from her eye and made its way down to the fox's fur. It landed there and became lost. This was the second and last time I have ever seen Aretha cry.

She cried for a long time.

I watched and waited for her to punch and slap and collapse her hands against my skin again, like that day at the cemetery.

She didn't.

Aretha wiped her eyes and lightly let one of her fingers take my hand.

Then. Right then.

    I fell in love with Aretha Jones. I looked over at her and my face became a slightly lighter shade of shade.

_____ Yes, I fell in love with Aretha that day. I've been dead ever since.

killer #6: happiness

It's strange sometimes, the things that make you happy. Just last night, I thought about how a moment of happiness undid my thoughts. I was emptied of everything, just for this one moment of happiness.

It concerns Aretha, naturally.

It also concerns the abode in which she lives.

This abode is often called an inconsolable, irretrievable shit-hole in which the girl I love and lust for resides.

The house has a dust job rather than a paint job.

It is made of your finest, decayed fibro.

Its kitchen floor is made of stale cornflakes that plaster themselves to your heels should you walk barefoot.

But it also contains the laughter of Aretha's chain-smoking, yet very approachable, mother. She obviously judges no one.

For her part, Aretha is pretty tidy.

Her room is up to speed, on account of the fact that she likes to sleep without dust settling in no uncertain terms in her mouth.

She has one bookshelf in her room.

She has several books on that bookshelf.

These books have brilliant titles like *Slugworth: The Untold Story*; *The Art of Taking the Jam Out of Someone's Donut*; and *Dancing in the Lounge Room*.

They stand like black, red, and gray soldiers.

One night, I picked up one of those books and found something written on the inside cover. It said this:

- Page 123, line 16.

Personally, I found this quite odd.

I proceeded to pick up the next book, which had nothing written on the inside cover. The one after that, however, had *three*:

- Page 87, line 1.
- Page 121, 3 lines from bottom.
- Page 146, line 6.

"What are these?" I asked Aretha.

She was lying on her mattress reading a book called *67 Things You Didn't Know About Raccoons*.

"Oh," she answered flippantly. "They're just mistakes."

This came as a shock. "Mistakes?"

"That's right — in the books."

Sure enough, I looked up one of the page numbers and found that two words at the top of the page were in the wrong order. It should have read, "I went all the way out to the snow-covered mansion" but it said, "I went the all way out to the snow-covered mansion."

"You collect mistakes in books?" I asked Aretha.

This time, she looked up. "Amongst other things."

*Other things?* I thought. "Like what?"

"You've played your flute forty-one times for me at the cemetery."

And she went on reading.

_____ Happiness is a nice killer. Polite. Well-mannered. You can have it delivered by a girl reading, stomach-down, elbow propped on her bed. But you have to be lucky.

# FILTHADELPHIA

### by Brian James

The bottle flew to its death, thirteen floors below, where glass doesn't meet so well with the asphalt world. It felt like a good toss leaving my hand, felt for sure like it would make it far enough past the side of the building to hit the street. No way to tell except for the sound, the sudden shattering noise or a frightful scream from a car's brakes as Will and I stay ducked down below the window. In case it hits anyone or anything, it's better not to be half hanging out the window with a big confession in the form of smiles on our faces.

A summer storm of stereos blasting out of windows and fans humming electric music into the Philly skyline isn't enough to muffle the shattering sounds of the bottle breaking and us losing our shit laughing. Bull's-eye.

"Holy shit, did you hear that?" Will asks once he's able to take a breath. I just nod and let my eyes go wide to show that I most certainly did hear it. I knew something glass would make a difference, I guess I just didn't figure it would make such a huge one going from a can to a bottle. Learn something new every time we play the throw-shit-out-the-window game.

My mom would say playing this game is a momentary lapse of reason. More like a momentary lapse in boredom though. Something to do at least. Something a little more interactive than television or video games since we've been doing that most of the afternoon, waiting around to find something else to do. Anything to relieve the symptoms and get a good laugh in.

Ryan's been on the phone for hours calling anyone and everyone to find us someone to hang out with. And by some-one, we mean *anyone* who has any weed.

It feels like Philly's been dry all summer. Like a desert wind came rolling down Broad Street and swept its way down every side road to leave us with nothing to smoke. Things get all stingy in the City of Brotherly Love when that happens. No one wants to let you know they have any. No one wants to share with you. No one wants you to find out where they got theirs, afraid you'll dry up the last source they got. Brotherly Love easily turns into Brotherly Greed.

Ryan comes into the room and sees us huddled on the floor with evil smiles on our faces like two little kids caught lighting matches. Will tells him we finally made the leap from mischief to danger and Ryan says he figured it was only a matter of time. It always happens that way, building up from tossing trash out his window to more menacing projectiles.

There's no sirens or screaming though, so we figure it's safe enough to take a peek. Survey the damage and that sort of thing.

We give a quick look at the mess. Spot a few glances up in our direction and dive back for cover in another fit of laughter before focusing on more serious business.

"Any luck?" I ask Ryan, not really counting on any but figuring it's polite to ask after all his efforts.

Ryan's got this way about him of never moving too far away from normal no matter how good or bad things might be at the time. Steady as he goes, just the way he was made. It's like that when he nods and says, "Yeah, actually Dave said he'd pick us up in his car and drive us out to Lee Street."

Lee Street means an instant score. It's like a drug supermarket but you need a car to gain access and get away fast.

Will nearly needs to be picked up from the floor when the news is dropped. Any of the rest of us, me or Kevin or Will even, we'd have come running into the room with our hands waving in the air. We'd have screamed out of the windows to shower the whole shitty town with the news, "WE'RE GETTING WEEED!" if for nothing else but to rub it in to any other sorry group of friends like us waiting around. Because having connections that come through is like a badge proving how much cooler you are.

"Are you serious? When's he coming?" I ask, ready to climb down the side of the building instead of taking the elevator if that's what needs to be done to make sure we don't miss good old Dave passing by in his beat-up junker.

"Uh, not sure. I guess we could wait outside. He should be here soonish," Ryan says like he's talking about shit that don't matter. Damn, sometimes I wish I could be that way. Not let anything show. Cool as anything.

We head straight for the elevator. Will and I are running on electricity, the promise of smoke in the veins enough to get us motivated for a back-roads drive through North Philly. Got to

29

gear up for the whole thing, because now that the arrangements have been made, there's the reality of the deal that has to go down, which has never been my favorite part of the routine. Any exchange has never really been something I look forward to, and Lee Street certainly isn't helping me feel any better. There's always a price to pay though for getting what you want, I suppose.

Getting in the elevator always makes me laugh a little. Every time I come or go from Ryan's, I can never get over that his parents actually have an apartment on the thirteenth floor or that the building even has one instead of skipping it and going from twelve to fourteen like most every building I've ever been in. I don't know why I get a kick out of it. I guess it's because it's like something I would do. Take something unlucky and wear it on purpose. Almost like making it good luck just by doing it. Rubbing everyone's stupid superstitions right in their faces, like saying to them I'm everything they're not and even their bad luck is good for me.

"Jesus Mice," Ryan says with a little smile as we head out of the lobby and into the muggy evening. "Did you throw my whole house out the window, Brendon?" he asks me and I just shrug and smile at the collection of soda cans, broken glass, and the last few bites of a cheesesteak that decorate the sidewalk and make Lombard Street a driving hazard for cars with weak tires.

"Nah, just the trash," I say with a smile of satisfaction, having left my mark on this filthy city at least for today.

Dave's car is like a billboard rolling down the street. Hardly an inch isn't covered with someone's graffiti tag. Spot it two blocks away. Hear it rattling from three. The whole thing is a fucking mess but whatever, if it's the mode of transportation I need to take, so be it. Just keep my fingers crossed hoping it don't break down along the way.

We run to meet him at the corner, trying to steer him away from the broken glass. It would be just the sort of luck we've had all summer if he got a flat on the bottle I fucking threw.

"Hey guys, climb in," Dave says, nodding in the direction of the passenger door. Like good soldiers, we follow orders and file in, Will and I filling the ranks in the back. Ryan's taking copilot privileges for masterminding the whole trip.

Dave's a good guy but he's crazy as shit.

Short-circuited in the head just a little, if you know what I mean. That's all right though. I mean, we all are, right? But something about Dave is a bit more off than the rest of us. It shows in his driving, too. Every stop sign is an adventure, every intersection like a test that I'm not so sure he's going to pass.

He catches my eye in the rearview mirror.

"Brendon, there's a lunch box back there on the floor somewhere." Not really a question or a command, but making it clear anyway that I'm supposed to find it. Making it clear he's watching me instead of the road until I do, so the motivation is pretty fucking strong to dig through the clothes and shit covering the floorboards at my feet.

"Power Rangers?" Holding it up and he says that's the one. Tells me to open up it and *power up*. Inside is a roach left over from God knows when. The paper burned and brown but enough weed left in between to show itself worthwhile to light.

It's basically just a tease when the taste touches my tongue before I pass it along to Will, but it's enough to get a little glare

31

in my eyes. When it comes around to me a second time it's enough to make me forget the death-trap ride we're taking and enjoy the feeling of the hazy wind blowing in the windows. Enough to make the whole city look dusted as we race through the crumbling streets with music loud enough to add to the chaos that surrounds us.

The streets get less familiar to me as we get farther north. I'm not lost or anything, just prefer not to spend my time around here. Not really my territory. A Center City boy doesn't do so well in these parts.

"Let's get our money together," Ryan says, volunteering himself to be the handler, which is just fine with me if it means I can sit in the back with my head down and mouth shut.

There's an unwritten rule about deals like this — that's never buy more than fifty dollars' worth. No matter how much all of us would like to beg, borrow, and steal our way to hundreds of dollars' worth to stock up for the summer. We know better. You ask for more than fifty and you leave there with no money and no weed. A gun pressed to your stomach as fast as the words come out of your mouth.

"We got forty-seven dollars," Ryan says, and since no one seems to be reaching for their pockets, I toss in the extra three and make a mental note that I get first hit based on that fact. "All set," and no sooner does he say it than we turn off Allegheny and into the belly of illegal substances.

Only one block long and a dead end to make sure there's only one way out, too. The perfect dealing spot, which is why the dealers are more plentiful here than pigeons in the park. Every stoop lining the sidewalk's littered with them. Not just the usual types, either, also grandmothers and grandkids.

Basically the scene is a family affair around these parts and that's what makes it more dangerous for kids like us rolling in because there's a fine line between being a customer and being a target. All of them against four of us.

There's a few cars in front of us being hounded by guys leaning in at every window. It's only seconds before the same happens to us. Two guys leaning half-in at every window of the car asking "what you want" and "how much" and fanning out little plastic bags of every known drug for us to see.

"We just want weed," Dave says.

The guy on Ryan's side tells us to pull up a few feet to where there's a trash can on the sidewalk. When he lifts the lid, we can see the whole thing is filled with bags of pot measured out in dollar amounts. It's like Santa's sack of toys and we're only hoping to get one little present without incident.

Too much to ask for though. I know for certain that it officially hasn't been our summer when we see the cop car behind us. I feel like I'm going to explode inside when it stops.

The dealer drops all that's in his hand onto Ryan's lap and moves away. Dave puts the car into drive and decides to test the engine if he needs to. I glance over at Will, who gives me a mirror image of my expression back. The old "oh shit, we're dead" look in our eyes.

I brace myself for the sirens but there aren't any. Looking out the back window, I see the cop isn't even following us. "He doesn't give a shit about us," I say, never having been so happy to be so meaningless as we head back to the real world. But not too far because we still got to figure out what the hell to do: whether we wait it out and go back for the pot, or take the four bags of coke the guy dropped in our car and never return.

Dave pulls into a gas station lot. Base camp for figuring things out.

Will doesn't want to go back at all. He figures even if the cop is gone, we still got four bags that we didn't pay for. "They're not going to let us give them back," he says, saying if we go back our money's just going to end up paying for what we already have anyway.

Dave's all for going back. "We can at least try," he says.

Ryan sort of shrugs, trying to stay neutral. Always on middle ground. Always able to see both sides, that's just how Ryan is.

"Fuck," I shout, because it's up to me. Swing vote and all that. And I know what the smart choice is, but I know the end result of that choice, too. Another night sitting around complaining how hot it is and how there's nothing to do. "Fuck it, let's go back."

Will shakes his head, blowing his breath out, angry. Looking at me to change my mind. And I know where he's coming from, but what the hell. I mean, if there's a cop car still there, we keep driving. It's worth a drive-by, since I still want weed. No matter how much free coke they dropped on us, I still want weed.

I climb back in the car and the rest of them do the same. Decision made.

No other cars are on the block when we turn onto Lee and we're spotted right away by the guy who tried to frame us with all he was carrying. "You guys," he says, and before he gets anything else out, Ryan hands back what's his. Tells him he forgot it, and I can't believe how he can be calm enough to be sarcastic.

The guy looks it over sort of surprised. Then nods and all is okay because there's a sort of code of ethics about drug deals.

Giving that back to him shows we play by the honor system and that seems to settle everything down.

The exchange we wanted in the first place is done quickly and we drive toward the high-rise lights towering in the distance.

As Ryan packs the bowl, Will gives me a look. And I know he's right. He doesn't have to say it. I know that maybe next time it doesn't work out quite in our favor. A run of luck never lasts. But that doesn't matter. This time it did.

A momentary lapse of boredom.

Deal with the crash after we fall down. A symptom of the modern age, I guess.

# PEOPLE WATCHING

## by Chris Wooding

I have to say, I'm not impressed. To start with, she's forty-three-point-two-five minutes late. Then when she does finally turn up, she's hardly the demure beauty I was hoping for. She looks like she swallowed a nailbomb and then fell into a pool of toxic sludge. It's the only way I can think of to explain the bruise-colored mascara, dyed hair sticking up all over the place, and spikes everywhere — one through her lower lip, one through each eyebrow like little horns, dozens down the arm of her leather jacket.

Everyone in the café notices her as she walks in, glancing over the rims of their lattes, possibly worrying that she might trip over and fatally wound someone.

I knew it. Never let your parents set you up on a blind date.

I manage to keep the horror off my face and rise to pull her chair out for her, the way a well-brought-up young man should. She stares at me blandly until I sit back down.

The coffee sippers watch with appalled fascination as this leather-and-steel-clad porcupine settles herself opposite me. Me, in my black silk shirt, my immaculately pressed trousers, my watch that costs more than the GNP of a small African country. I'm only thankful I didn't ask her to meet me somewhere classy. To think, I was worried that she might feel intimidated.

"I see you came as Medusa," I say gallantly, forcing a smile.

"I see you came as yourself," she replies, and somehow her tone makes it an insult.

Her eyes flick from me to the glass wall on our left. We're on the second floor, overlooking a busy street in Ealing. It's a gray London day, clouds pressing down hard on the capital. Shoppers walk back and forth, exploring the exciting opportunities afforded by dozens of chain stores selling precisely nothing of interest.

I sit back and drum my fingers on the table. "Should we pretend to make an effort?" I ask.

She looks me up and down as if I'm a tower of radioactive excrement orbited by vastly mutated flies.

"Let's not and say we did," she says.

We sit in silence for a time. Below us, a squad of chuggers chase after shoppers with inviting smiles, trying to lure them into conversation. "Charity muggers" are a fascinating new stage in humankind's development, beings whose only purpose appears to be infuriating passersby into pledging monthly donations to their cause. Perhaps they do not imagine that every person they talk to has already been approached by six other chuggers farther down the street.

I observe a woman laden with shopping bags who is being dogged by two screaming children and three competing chuggers. She has gone red and has begun to shake. Wise passersby are giving her a wide berth.

The waitress glides into view next to our table.

"Is it ready to order, please?" she says in the teeth-grindingly mangled grammar of one newly arrived in the country.

"I'll have a double soy-milk macchiato, please," I say crisply.

"Coffee," says my date, not looking up from the street.

"Americano, espresso, moccachino?"

She turns away from the window, kohl-stained eyes shadowing a basilisk glare. "Coffee," she says in a voice that could pulverize diamonds. The waitress quails and retreats.

Below us, a tall man flings himself against the closing doors of a bus. The driver stares at him for a full thirty seconds as he hammers on the door, then drives away, leaving the would-be passenger to make obscene gestures and slander the driver's mother.

I decide to make an effort to salvage the situation, if only so I can look Father in the eye and tell him I tried. Quite heroic of me, really. I'm desperately picky when it comes to girls. They're so illogical, unreasonable, *emotional*. But it's been a long time since my last date — a *really* long time — and I think Father's getting a bit worried.

"Do you like them?"

"Sorry?" she says, with a long sigh of such unutterable desolation that I can't help but think of foggy graveyards, ancient tombs, ruined cities. Her sullen gloom is infectious.

"The people. Do you like them?"

Her gaze tells me how banal she thinks my question is.

"I hate them," she says.

"Why?"

38

She stirs, sighs again, letting me know what a huge effort it is to talk to me. "They used to ride across the plains on horses," she says. "They used to fight and die for an idea. They used to cast themselves into the unknown in search of adventure. Wars raged and empires fell for the love of a woman." She casts her eyes down. "Look at them now. The greatest challenge they face is whether to buy organic or stone-baked bread at the supermarket. They're soft. Bored. Weak."

I blink. I'm rather surprised at the venom in her voice.

"I suppose *you* like people," she says with a sneer.

"Certainly not."

"Really?" She's suspicious. Thinks I'm just agreeing with her to be pleasant. As if I'd stoop to currying favor with someone as wretched-looking as her.

"Absolutely. Look at the mess they make. Everywhere I go — graffiti, litter, burst pipes. Fumes, car alarms, chewing gum on the pavement, those little red rubber bands the postmen leave all over the place. Dirt, filth, muck. Look!"

Across the street, a pair of weasel-faced inbreds are sloping out of a fast-food restaurant. They pull the wrappers from their burgers and throw them casually onto the ground.

"You know what this place needs?" She leans forward, fiddling with her matted hair, and for the first time she half smiles. I see a glint of mischief in her eye.

"What?"

"Snipers."

"Snipers?"

She points to the rooftops. I follow the line of her finger. "There, and there. First offense is a warning shot. Second

39

through the back of the knee. Three strikes, a nice clean one through the head."

"For *littering*?" I gasp.

"Right," she says. "You gotta admit, it'd make them think twice."

The waitress has appeared with our drinks and is eyeing us with concern. She's caught the tail end of our conversation and is not keen on the idea of giving caffeine to an obvious psychopath. I notice she's a little hasty as she puts down the cups and scurries away.

My date is watching me, a challenge in her gaze. Waiting to see how I've taken what she said. She likes to shock, I see.

I motion with my hand to the window. "The man in the plaid jacket," I say. She scans the street, locates him. He cuts a ridiculous figure: fat, balding, middle-aged, cheeks puffing as he hurries to some undoubtedly pointless destination.

"See him?" I ask.

She makes an affirmative noise. A moment later, he catches his toe on a paving stone and falls full-length onto his belly. Change scatters from his pockets and rolls away in meandering arcs across the pavement. Passersby either suppress their laughter or walk on past, pretending it never happened.

"Nobody's stopping," she says. There's a kind of fascination in her voice all of a sudden.

"Did you really think they would?" I ask as the man levers himself up, face flushed beetroot red, clutching his chest. He hurries away without even picking up his money.

"How about that one?" she says, sipping her coffee and indicating someone with a flick of her eyes.

It's a skinny young man in a pink T-shirt and outsize ripped jeans, hair in an elaborately designed mess. He's spent a lot of money to look that scruffy.

His belt comes loose, his jeans fall around his ankles, and he falls in a heap in front of a gang of teenage girls. They screech with laughter until a salvo of pigeon excrement spatters all over their tracksuits. The bombers soar away, following a tight V formation not usually employed by London's famed Rats of the Sky.

Across the table from me, she laughs into her coffee and then chokes, spraying the window. I watch her indulgently, a faint smile on my lips.

"I knew there had to be a reason pigeons existed." She chuckles.

"You try," I say.

"You don't know my parents. They'll be so mad." She grins.

"Oh, come on. Let it out a little."

She surveys the street. "How about Slick, over by the bank?"

It's a man in a suit, immaculately groomed, probably in real estate or law or banking or another one of the criminal professions. She's testing me. He's neat as a pin; she wants to see if I'll object.

"Be my guest," I say, and he vanishes down an open manhole that certainly wasn't there half a second before.

I cackle in appreciation. Her selection of misfortune did have a certain wicked charm about it. Exactly three-point-six seconds later, two big red buses collide head-on outside the window with an almighty smash.

41

People in the café begin to scream. Chairs screech as people stand up and run to the window, crowding uncomfortably near to me.

My date and I watch casually as people run toward the crashed buses, pulled to disaster like predators to a carcass.

"Now you're just showing off," she says.

She clicks her fingers and the road splits lengthways, a chasm opening along the High Street. Cars swerve and tip, people stagger and plunge into the crevasse. Bright magma spews out in pretty red fans, geysering into the air, spattering the shoppers as they shriek and flee this way and that. The façade of a bank crumbles, slumping into the street, burying a gang of teenagers who were busy filming the carnage with the cameras on their mobile phones.

The people in the café are in hysterics now, fleeing for the stairs, babbling prayers. My date and I sip our coffees.

"Haven't had this much fun since Atlantis," she says.

"You were at Atlantis?"

"Sure. Weren't you?"

"I was visiting a plague of locusts on Egypt."

"That was you? I always did like the locusts. Better than the frogs or the boils."

"Very kind of you to say. Might I ask why you chose to appear in such an . . . interesting body?"

"I thought it'd annoy you."

"Oh, it does."

"Good."

I watch the chaos below, as a seventy-foot-high golem of lava and rock clambers out of the chasm in the High Street and starts throwing cars around.

"It's about time they got a bit of a shake-up," I say, tapping my teeth with a nail.

"Our parents are *really* going to kill us when they find out," she says, but she's watching me with a gaze that can only be described as ravenous. And, well, a boy can't help but find that kind of passion just a little bit attractive.

"Children will play," I say.

She reaches across the table and takes my manicured hand.

"You think this might work out?"

"Oh, yes," I say. "Want to flood Holland next?"

"Can we set the Midwest on fire first?"

I raise her hand to my lips and kiss her knuckle.

"For you, my dear, anything."

# MY BOYFRIEND REFUSES TO SPEAK IN IAMBIC PENTAMETER

### by Billy Merrell

CHARACTERS

JEROME
JEFF
MOM
DAD
JEFF'S MOTHER
JEFF'S STEPFATHER

ACT I

*(The curtain is lifted, revealing a white room. It is empty and its walls are blank. Some music begins faintly in the background.*

*JEROME enters, carrying a box. He puts a poster on the wall. It is bright and colorful. He hangs some photographs. Another poster. A shelf. As he continues*

*his work, the lights fade. A scrim is lowered between*
*him and the audience. The music continues.)*

(SCENE: *After a moment the scrim is lifted and the*
*lights rise, revealing* JEROME *alone in his room. It no*
*longer looks like a set. It is a room.*

JEROME *sits on the floor, photographs and magazines*
*laid out around him. He cuts images out of each and*
*collages them onto an old guitar. He works slowly. The*
*music fades into the background.)*

I know it's real, but realize it's not you
who's here to help me see how well it works
without much ~~pain~~
        work, the way it follows through
without requiring that I follow ~~you~~.
                  Look,
at first it felt like we were tied together,
so if you walked out angry, I did too.
You stormed around; I learned to ~~fear your weather~~
               notice whether
you ~~wanted~~ me to cure or comfort you.
   needed
I thought you thought that love would be a chore
the way you roll your eyes at photos of us,
but now I see you've always wanted more
than what your parents
         had.

(JEROME *pastes the last of the images onto the*
*guitar, then stands to look at it from farther away.)*

    And maybe you won't notice,
but there is one for every day we've shared.

45

*(He begins to clean up.)*

It seems my heart has always been prepared.

*(The lights fade to black.)*

*(SCENE: Out of the darkness, a faint blue light rises, revealing two boys' faces. They are sitting on the bed next to each other, close enough to be holding hands. They're watching a movie. The light flickers brighter revealing the two, each looking up at the clock occasionally, discreetly, so the other doesn't notice. JEROME smiles when JEFF catches him. He opens a window and a single firefly enters.)*

It seems my heart has always been prepared
for someone to sneak in, despite bad luck.
We each had closed our mouths, been truth-then-dared:
the next thing that we knew our mouths weren't shut.
And neither were our minds —

*(One, then another firefly blinks in through the open window. As the boys sit there, several more crowd in. When the clock finally strikes midnight, there are countless fireflies above their heads. JEROME pauses the movie.)*

          I'd always known,
and now I have to wonder how much time
I would have spent denying it, alone,
if you weren't there to put your mouth to mine.

*(JEROME tells JEFF to close his eyes and reaches silently under the bed. The fireflies surround them.)*

Sometimes I laugh, remembering your face
when I first pulled my lips away and smiled.

46

You gave yourself away, gave me a place
to put myself — at least for some short while.
And nearly one year later, here we are:
your eyes still closed, me holding your guitar.

(JEROME *tells* JEFF *he can open his eyes. The lights
fade, except for the fireflies, which hover faithfully.
When the lights rise,* JEFF *is the one holding the
guitar.* JEROME *stands facing him, holding a card
that reads "You Make Me Happier Than Words
Can Say.")*

My eyes are closed. You're holding your guitar.
(I've never felt so stupid in my life.)
I spent forever; you bought me a card
and wrote in it *You're great! Yours truly, Jeff*.
The thing is, I don't care how much you spent,
but all you did is pick it from a shelf
while I spent nights recalling how it went:
~~our kiss, our year~~.
You didn't even make the thing yourself.
How lame am I for thinking that you cared,
for thinking this all means as much to you
when clearly you don't love me — or are you scared
to show me how you feel, to feel it too?
But as I go to say it, my eyes open.
I'm never sure when mine's the heart that's broken.

(JEFF *sets the guitar on the bed and turns away.*
JEROME *reaches for him and* JEFF *hides his face,
then wipes his eyes and thanks him.*)

My heart, it seems, is not the heart that's broken.
To see his face, to see him standing there,
all guilt and puppy frown. I tell him, *Look,
it's no big deal*. But he's beyond repair.

47

*(A firefly leaves through the window.)*

JEFF:
Gosh, you're cheesy. What?
Well, I gonna go. Just gotta . . .
but I'll see you tomorrow, right?

> *(JEROME nods.*

> JEFF *stands, steps toward him, and, hesitating, kisses
> him goodbye.)*

It's not the kind of kiss I'd ever want:
I feel it come and go before it starts,
his lips so tight with tension that I can't
feel him behind them, let alone the ~~love~~
                             part
of him I'm kissing. Strangers suddenly,
no history to hold us in our touch.
I want to say, *Don't go. It's done*, and be
contented, maybe, having said as much,

> *(They hug briefly.)*

but my throat is sore, my mouth as dry as ice.
Somehow I stand there, ~~silent~~
                        breaking his heart twice.

> *(As the door closes behind* JEFF, *the stage begins to
> rotate, revealing a hall, then another room on the
> opposite side of the wall.* JEROME *opens his bedroom
> door and the fireflies swarm the hallway, then follow
> him to his parents' bedroom, where the couple lies
> reading in bed.*

JEROME *knocks on the door. The lights again fade.
Except for the fireflies — they flood the unlit room
until the lights rise.)*

JEROME:
But I just stood there, breaking his heart twice
while he walked out, my present in his hand.
I want to call him and apologize, but . . .

MOM:
Well tell him that. I'm sure he'll understand.

JEROME:
I guess, but you don't know him like I do.
He acts all tough, but really he's . . . well . . . not.
Besides, I feel there's something here to prove,
like he should call me first. Is that a lot
to ask? I mean, I love him, but come on.
The least that he could do is maybe call
and, well, be nicer. I don't know. I'm done
feeling like crap when none of it's my fault.

DAD:
Well if you love him, and I know you do,
that seems to me the harder thing to lose.

*(The fireflies scatter from the stage, forming loose con-
stellations above the audience.)*

*(SCENE: A Nightmare:*

*The stage is dark when* JEROME *walks to the edge.
Soon it is lit as if by moonlight. A single beam cuts
sharply through onto the bedside table, making the
edge of a phone just visible.* JEROME *sits at the edge
of the bed.)*

It seems to me the hardest thing to lose
is loss itself. No matter what I try,
it will not leave me lossless.

> (JEROME *nods and puts his legs beneath the covers.*
> JEFF *walks in, but not into the light. He steps up to*
> JEROME *for a kiss. But where are the fireflies?*)

I refuse
to be the one forever left behind —
be it a boy who takes his touch away,
be it a shape I never knew was bliss:

> (JEROME *kisses* JEFF.)

I pull my tired arms from around his waist,
and find them hanging empty without his
tangled there too. Unraveling from our source —
What source is that? Unbound, unbent. I gave
my answer to the ghost.

> (JEFF *fades as if he had always been a shadow.*)

He said to force
his love is not to love him truly, bravely.
And as I woke the room around me broke.
There was no mouth, but it was you who spoke.

> (JEROME *reaches for the phone. Blackout.*)

> (SCENE.)

It was your mouth but it was them who spoke:
you said you couldn't talk so late. I knew
they sat there, listening, ~~amused~~

50

~~and you~~
         and me, your joke —

         *(JEROME puts the receiver to his chest, then lifts it
         back to his ear.)*

I said goodnight, unsatisfied. ~~But you . . .~~

         *(He hangs up.)*

                    It goes
like this: first heart, then touch, then fever breaks.
So that when I'm left alone with you, I wonder
when are we actually alone? For the sake
of ~~argument~~
      honesty, let's say whose spell you're under:
It's simple how she does it, turns on me,
as if I made you how you are, as if
I turned some switch and lit the fire, free
of consequences: tongue and lip.

         *(Again, the stage rotates, this time revealing JEFF'S
         house. He sits at a table with JEFF'S MOTHER. She
         smokes while he plays chords on his new guitar.)*

It hurts to see ~~the difference~~
               their reasoning, I guess.
To hear your parents say they know what's best.

         *(As the curtain is lowered, one can hear JEROME shut
         his bedroom door. The music continues long after the
         houselights have come on.)*

INTERMISSION

51

ACT II

*(Before the curtain is lifted or the houselights signal a
return, one can hear* JEROME *from backstage.)*

JEROME:
I heard your parents say they know what's best,
but Jeff, they don't. And even if you claim
you don't buy into what they're saying —

*(The audience members quietly, awkwardly, find their
seats. The houselights fade.)*

                                    Yes,
it's true. My parents smothered me. But blame's
a stupid waste of time. I'm telling you.
Who cares whose fault is whose, or even why?
Half the time it's messy and the truth
will get you nowhere, so don't waste your time —
I'm sorry, but it's true. And your folks
may think they're right, but you can't safely say
their love is half as great as ours. No jokes.
I'm serious. Don't look at me that way.
It's just that if you're happy, why's it matter?
And they'll get over it, at least they better.

*(The curtain rises.*

JEROME *walks onstage. A spotlight follows him as he
finds his seat. The edges of his surroundings are gilded
by the amber light.)*

~~And they'll~~ get over it. ~~At least they better.~~
But I'll                          I always do.

52

*(A little more of his surroundings are revealed: rows of desks, all empty.)*

~~Alone~~ in ~~my~~ room,
  A kid    a       I watch the teacher teach,
but can't pretend to hear her. Test of truth,
test of sweetness in the soil. I reach
in my bag and find your card once more, and read
it slow, in case I missed some subtle cure.

*(JEROME reaches into his backpack with both hands, and when he pulls them out, they are clasped together. A faint light held between his palms.)*

Again, I feel I'm forcing you: your sea
the voice in every shell, your romance more
than the sum of its parts. Forgive me for my needs;
my clinginess is more than I can tame.
~~My breath still held~~
~~Your voice.~~

*(When JEROME opens his hands, he reveals a single firefly. Freed, it remains in his hand, the light pulsing.)*

That ringing bell, it punctuates the scene,
but it's not time itself, not by that name.
I wondered at the love left in us all;
I saw us, each, who wander, hall to hall.

*(As JEROME stands, the stage begins to rotate. The firefly remains calm in his cupped palm. He walks to a door, dreamily. He steps through it. On the other side, we see JEFF and his family waiting at a table. When JEROME closes the door behind him, the stage lights brighten suddenly. The family looks up.*

JEROME *puts his backpack down and awkwardly takes an empty seat.)*

The only thing that's worse than coming late
is barely being noticed at the table.
I push the peas in circles on my plate,
wishing we weren't just sitting, watching cable.

(JEFF'S STEPFATHER *tries repeatedly to change the channel during commercials, but the television doesn't respond to the remote.)*

JEFF'S STEPFATHER:
Why isn't the clicker working?

JEFF'S MOTHER:
Did you check the batteries, Hal?

(*Eventually the show comes back on and he is content again.* JEFF'S MOTHER *doesn't look up from her plate;* JEFF *smiles at* JEROME *occasionally, but mostly watches the show.*)

But why the silence? Why the blunt refusal
to look me in the eyes, to ask a question?
I sit and ~~wonder~~
           study them — like why'd she choose Hal
if he won't give her what she needs? A lesson
for me: if Jeff can't ~~give me~~
                    ~~tell me~~
                         show me what I need,
how long should I hold on to habit's love —
if I can't say with certainty it's me
he loves? But habit only. It's not enough
to love him; I need more than constancy:
I need to know he knows that he needs me.

54

*(JEROME smiles uncomfortably, then stands. Only
JEFF seems to notice. The boys walk to JEFF'S room
as the stage rotates, revealing it. The parents finish
their dinner as they disappear into the darkness.*

*The two stand quietly. JEFF sits on the bed, but
JEROME doesn't follow him.)*

I wonder at the love left in us all:
I move the papers, touch the photographs,
and wonder what is left — if ~~nights like this~~
                  I should fall
or catch me while I can. How much is left
~~and do I hold it all~~
and is there love for me in you, addressed
and ready to pour out — is it pouring now?
Is this all I get?

               *(JEROME turns his back to JEFF, pretends to look at
the pictures in a SEVEN WONDERS OF THE
WORLD wall calendar.)*

        Are you the best
there is for me? Is what I want ~~to know~~
                     ~~a show~~
                  a tower
in a field? More love than enough? Are you ~~here~~
                              hear-
ing me?

JEFF:
Jerry — what's wrong?
You've been weird since dinner.

    A statue where some broken body stood?

JEFF:
Jerry? Come on.

JEROME:
I didn't know your dad would buy us beer.

JEFF:
Pretty cool, huh? Since it's a special occasion and all.

> (JEFF *stands and steps toward* JEROME, *who pushes him away.*)

JEROME:
You mean you told them?! How'd they take it? Good?

JEFF:
Dude. I told you. They've known
longer than I have. They'll just need some time
getting used to it. Not all parents are
cheerleaders for gayness.

JEROME:
I can't believe you'd say that. And tonight!
I mean what a gesture: how 'bout start a fight?!

JEFF:
Okay, Jerry. What is this really about?

> (JEFF *tries again to hug* JEROME. *He tries to push him off, but* JEFF *won't let him.*)

I want the gesture — mometary ~~hand~~
                              stroke
~~of hand in mine~~ —
I want to see the pulleys and the cords,

that lavishly wild machine of love, bespoke,
~~mined~~
made mine by longing. And you: severely bored.

(JEROME *begins to explain.*)

How can you say you love me — do you really? —
when you can't ~~shoulder~~
                    show her, wholly, who I am?
Unbridled scope or scale, ~~unbroken trellis~~
                            the kind of feeling
you can't just ~~say~~
                write without disturbing the calm
~~of a blank page~~
~~of sense~~.
You think I speak like this because I can?
~~Because without the beat there is no heart?!~~
My form is not my structure, it's my mode:
it's how I handle ~~love~~
                    truth; it's how I ~~find it~~
                                    land
squarely inside ~~the~~ self,
                my      honestly ~~wrote~~
                                    ~~wrought~~
                                    ~~written~~
                                        found!
It isn't that I long for you to sing,
it's that I long for care in everything.

Because without the beat, there is no heart.
And sentiments seem strung along on lines
of half-felt courtesies — when what I want
is romance strung upon a blooming vine —
not for the flowers, but for their opening.

In love, any truth is kind because it's ~~true~~
                                        real.
And any lie is worse ~~because it's not~~.
                    I hope you sing —
but not because you think I want you to.
Because you can't hold back, so much unsaid,
because you've looked so deeply in my eyes
that you can't see much else. Because instead
of wanting your life the same, you realize
that maybe it can never be again.
~~And that's okay.~~

                    *(JEFF nods, but JEROME shakes his head no.)*

JEROME:
Remember how you said we should stay friends —

JEFF:
Okay, now you're just pissing me off!
Are you even interested in giving me a chance?
Has it occurred to you that maybe this is all
harder for me than it is for you? I mean,
I'm trying to be romantic. I gave you that stupid card
because it was in iambic pentameter on the front
or whatever. I thought you'd think it was funny.

                    *(The two stand there in silence for several moments.)*

JEFF:
Well, this was supposed to be a surprise,
but I don't know how to even bring it up.
I tried to write you a song or whatever.
But it's really stupid. I mean REALLY.

*(JEFF goes to his closet and pulls out the guitar. He sits next to JEROME and begins to play the chords. He clears his throat. JEROME laughs a little, though he is already crying. JEFF gets to the part of the song where he should begin singing, but chickens out. He begins the intro again. On the second try, he begins singing.)*

JEFF:
Remember when I said we should stay friends
Because I didn't want to say good-bye.
I take it back; I simply can't pretend
A friendship holds as much as you and I

Hold daily: holding hands or holding still,
Holding each other late into the night —

*(As he sings, the fireflies in the audience return to the stage. They form a bright cloud above the song.)*

Or holding tight, so patiently, until
That moment we're together, the timing right . . .

So I'm not as good at metaphors as you,
Or saying often that I love you still
But you know what I'm saying when I do . . .

Whisper in your ear or tell you softly,
Even if what I'm saying isn't poetry
And I mess up everything, just like me.

*(JEROME laughs louder, wiping his face.)*

My songs are quiet, wordless rants at best,
because I'm scared to lose all that we've made.

And so I hold my cards up to my chest
and question every bet or pair I've played.

So I'm not as good at metaphors as you,

> (JEFF'S *voice cracks a little and they both laugh.*
> JEFF *rolls his eyes.*)

Or singing, even. How embarrassing.
But you know what I'm saying when I do . . .

Whisper in your ear or tell you, my voice cracking,
Even if what I'm saying isn't poetry
And I mess up everything, and it isn't perfect. And I'm sorry.

> (*The lights fade as the boys embrace. The fireflies
> surround them, so brightly the audience must look
> away. When they look back, the couple is gone.*)

JEROME:
Don't be.

JEFF:
Happy anniversary, Jerome.

> (SCENE: *A voice. Who knows which? The curtain is
> lowered slowly. Some chords begin. The audience
> remains in their seats after the houselights have
> come on.*)

I'll never know what love is like for you,
how much or little you have found in it,
or if, one morning, we might learn some truth
and let it break this spell we wrestle with —
as some astonished child would do, his heart
still easy to unset, his mind made up

as soon as it's unmade: ~~his parent's part~~
                              his parents having parted,
~~placed their bets~~.
Some day some force may come and interrupt
what calm we've found, but I can't worry now
about the end, still busy with beginning.
I see us through new eyes and wonder how
it is we have such lasting. ~~We're on a roll.~~
                              My God, we're winning.
The boy I was wants only to ~~find~~ love,
                              make
to know it's real and realize that's enough.

# KATIE JAMES BEATS THE BLUES

### by Kristen Kemp

The text message says: *U, me, 2nite. Cant wait.*

I can wait. When Blue and I got together, at least it was a beginning. This evening will be our finale, but not so grand. I flip my cell closed and throw it in my backpack, hoping it will break.

"Goodness gracious, Katie, you're going to give yourself a panic attack," Matt says as we turn onto the street of the public library. "And your phone doesn't deserve that kind of abuse."

"You want me to take advice from you?" I ask my reinstated best friend, who's had this body-plus-clothing makeover that still freaks me out. First, he had a popular girlfriend who styled and sexed him up; now he has a workout-freak girlfriend who bulks and sexes him up. He's got this great posture, and I'm still a slouch (but I do dress better than I used to). Everything was fine until we kissed twice, six months ago. He was like a favorite sweatshirt; now he's an itchy wool sweater I don't want to toss out. It doesn't help that his girlfriend Juliana is a b-word, and I can't be blamed for telling him so. I swear I'm not jealous. I just don't like it when she tells him what to do, uses him as a chauffeur, and borrows his money but forgets to pay him back.

"Didn't Juliana tell you to lose weight yesterday while we were all ordering dessert?" I am in a foul mood, and I'm walking too quickly in front of him, and I really should be sweeter because of the reinstatement of our best friendship and all. But she did tell him he was fat, and he just said, "You're right," while the rest of us gasped.

Matt gives me a dirty look as we get closer to the entrance.

"I'm sorry," I say, making eye contact with him. "It's just . . . it's just —"

"Blue, I know." We plan regular outings like this, hoping that one of them will finally repair our platonic relationship. Today we're on the hunt for free self-help books. He wants one called *Stumbling on Happiness*. I'm after *The Highly Sensitive Person*.

"He does love you, by the way," Matt adds softly, as if the l-word is vulgar or taboo.

"I don't think so." Now I can't look at him. My boyfriend wants us to stay together, and while that sounds like a good idea, a few obstacles stand in our way. First of all, he's going to San Diego State University. That is exactly 2,110.7 miles from my house, and my car is thirty-nine years old. Second, he's never uttered the l-word. We're so great together, but the greatness is so not acknowledged.

It's a long story, but our relationship began at senior prom in May. He arrived at my house to take me in my old purple Beetle, even though I had broken out in hives earlier that day. He scratched my splotches when I was too uncomfortable to dance. During slow songs, he slid the spaghetti straps off my dress — not in a horndoggy way, but in a tender way because there were big welts underneath. (I so cannot eat chocolate without needing an EpiPen, but that's exactly what I did on the afternoon before my senior prom.) When the slow songs came on — the ones that made the drunk girls cry — he pulled our chairs really close together, facing each other, so we could kinda-sorta sit and dance. The way he kissed me when the bass came on made me want to run to the drugstore for condoms. It wasn't the most comfortable four hours I've ever spent in a formal gown, but it was definitely the most romantic. Almost every day since, I've seen him. He holds my hand in that fingers-interlocked way. My ex-boyfriend Paul, who I was with from eighth to eleventh grades, would only hold my hand palm-to-palm. Paul used to tell me all the time how he felt — "I love you; you're so beautiful." Blue doesn't, but he's more caring, the kind of guy who brings me caffeine on nights before big tests. We do things together I wouldn't consider with Paul (yes, *that*). But the l-word? It just hasn't been said. And I can't say it first because then I will never know if he said it back because he felt obligated or if he really meant it. Or worse — what if he doesn't say it back?

Matt and I see the revolving door in front of the grubby steps at the library entrance. There's a woman who looks like she needs a home reading *Cat Fancy* upside down. I am suddenly attacked by a twenty-five-year-old man who's holding two cases of M&M's.

He gets way up in my face and yells, "Help our school's basketball team get uniforms. Just two-fifty for candy." I'm trying not to look at him, which is easy because the scar on his forehead is scary.

"If I had any money, would I be coming here?" I say, speeding up and wishing I were the kind of person who could tell him to stick his boxes up his a-hole. There's no way that guy is in high school or on any basketball team. I suddenly wish I had stayed at home alone in the dark with my cell phone turned off. But getting any peace and quiet there is impossible because my mom and stepdad are blasting *The Sound of Music* and drinking Bud Light. (They're on diets.)

"It's just two-fifty, miss!"

Matt's ahead of me, safely passing through the revolving glass doors. When I'm halfway in, halfway out, Scarface yells again: "I said miss, not *BITCH*!"

I stop and turn around, nearly getting tangled in the door. I give him the evilest eye I can manage, which freaks him out because my pupils are really weird. They're kind of purple even without contacts. He steps back while I run in. Matt goes full circle through the door till he is face-to-face with the candy man.

I'd never heard Matt say the f-word, but he does along with another word, "off." The *Cat Fancy* lady laughs, and Matt grabs her magazine and gives it back to her right side up. He storms into the library.

"Thanks." I'm staring at him, noticing for the first time how he looks more like a twenty-year-old man than like the twelve-year-old boy I've always kept in my mind. When we were twelve, I'd head up trees first and he'd be scared but follow me. The only thing I know for sure is that nothing stays the same.

"You can pay me back tonight," Matt answers, asking a skin-and-bones, two-centuries-old librarian for "some book called *Stumbling on Happiness*."

My heart sinks as I once again think of tonight, the last night, with Blue.

* * *

Yes, we are having a party — the best kind, with just best friends, booze, and a basement. But I am not happy. I am so not happy. Blue's going to follow his free-spirit hippie dreams to California. Matt, rehabilitated Shitville geek, is headed to Georgetown in Washington, D.C., even though he wanted to go to nearby Franklin College in Indiana. Mr. Class President and all-around-awesome guy Kevin is going an hour and a half away to University of Kentucky. Frankie, the jokester, is headed off to France to find not only herself but as many pretty lesbians as she can. Me, I'm staying in Shitville. Everyone else is leaving to go on life-changing adventures while I help Vicki J., my severely irritating redneck mother who I love more than Chinese food, wash dye out of ladies' hair in the salon she runs in our basement. I'm tired of having fingernails the color of baby poop. I'm tired of Vicki J. lecturing me about beauty school or enrolling in the Coast Guard or taking modeling classes. I loathe fixing myself up; I can only doggy paddle; and I'm short.

This is my own fault. I meant to apply for college. But now it's August, and I just didn't get around to it. My grades were mostly Bs; I could've gotten into local schools. I just have no clue what to do with my life. I do not enjoy school, so I can't imagine *paying* to take classes for four more years. I have been spending the summer putting off plans as if the end of August would never come. And as if high school would be enough to carry me through the rest of my life.

There is only one other person staying: Cherry, the slutty-but-lovable cheerleader who took Matt's virginity, will be attending beauty school in September. She's Kevin's girlfriend, and they plan to stay together despite the long distance and despite the fact that he's premed at U of K. They're crazy because all they do is get jealous of other girls and boys, fight madly, then get busy in closets and under picnic tables making up. She thinks we're friends, and we kind of are — except that she took Matt's virginity, adding to the general weirdness between him and me.

I really wish Matt wasn't going to Georgetown just because his mother is making him be a lawyer. He wanted to major in elementary education at Franklin. I don't know why he doesn't follow his heart. I imagine following Juliana has something to do with it — she's also headed to D.C., to American University to study music while Matt studies her.

The reason I've procrastinated all summer is I've been deliriously happy. Blue and I have gone everywhere in my Beetle, from Monmouth Cave to King's Island to Graceland. When we haven't been together, I've been with the rest of our odd crew of popular people plus geeks. We've had pizza-eating contests, snuck wine coolers by the Ohio River, and danced in the middle of the street on a gingham tablecloth in Cherry's busy neighborhood at midnight. Tonight we're planning on doing the same thing in front of Kevin's house. (His parents are in Florida.)

If I even go, that is.

"Goddammit, girl!" says Vicki J. over the lyrics from the TV. "Maybe Bob needs to buy you a trip to some all-inclusive resort in the Caribbean. Maybe you just need to get away for a little while. Be alone, figure out what you want to do with your life, and find a nice young Jamaican in the meantime, mon."

"I *have* a boyfriend," I remind her. She had a very hard

time committing to Bob before they got married last year, even though he loves her more than the oxygen he breathes, and she loves him as much as peroxide.

"Your boyfriend is a-leavin' you, honey. We can't dance around it. I know it hurts, but it don't have to hurt for so very long," she says. "Go to Jamaica and find a hottie. Stella got her groove back, so my Katie James can beat the blues."

I look at her with an evil eye, and she turns away laughing.

"Hi, sweetheart," Bob says, drinking his Bud Light from a chilled glass instead of using one of Vicki's can huggies. He gives me a squeeze. He's lost twenty pounds over the summer, which is good because he has about a hundred more to go. He's a great daddy since my own died so long ago. He would totally pay for a trip for me if I wanted it. He owns this company that builds things, but Mom and I hate gold diggers, so we rarely let him spoil us the way he wants to.

"Well, we'll talk tomorrow if you're ripe for talking," my mother says as she steams vegetables for Bob. "I know you've got your thang to do."

Vicki J. knows Blue and I have had sex, and she knows that I'll stay the night at Kevin's. She knows I like Big Red spiked with amaretto, and she doesn't mind what I do as long as I'm with this great group of friends, and as long as I don't drive.

I head to my room to straighten my curly, curly hair so I can look as hot as possible for our party tonight. I ordered Blue a cake that says *San Diego State*, and I have to go to the party, I guess, or else he'll never get to eat it.

My room is this peachy color, and it's so high school, and I'm finally feeling like I'm so *not* high school for the first time ever in my life. I finish putting on mascara, the only makeup I'll agree to wear, and I hear him at the door of our cozy ranch house. I tie my cool Skechers that actually look good with skirts. I feel warm and scared and sad all over. I cannot wait to see him, and I cannot imagine him leaving me here. I run into the living room, and Blue kisses me even though my parents are right there.

It hurts, though.

"You smell amazing," he says, whisking me down the hall even though I don't have my purse.

Once we're in the driveway, he hugs me supertight, and I hug him back for as long as I can because then maybe he won't leave in the morning.

He hands me a roll of toilet paper when we get into my Beetle. He leaves his Mustang at my house because we like my purple love buggy better.

"What the hell?" I say, figuring a roll of toilet paper is *not* an acceptable bouquet.

"This is from the time I surprised you in the bathroom at school. Remember? You went in; I followed you. I asked you out; you said no."

"You kept a roll of toilet paper?" I say, melting because I love his dark wavy hair, his blue eyes, the way his hand gently turns the dials on the car radio, pressing the buttons so the decals will never come off.

"Open the glove box," he says as he shifts — he loves to drive, and I let him. He also fiddles with the radio and stops at a rap station. I love rap; he hates it.

I see a necklace made out of leather cord with a thumbnail-size piece of turquoise on it. I wonder how he snuck it into my Beetle and how long it's been in there.

"Wear it when we're not together?" he asks. "You're going to forget me."

My heart almost comes out of my mouth in the form of a really embarrassing, totally gushing, "I love you!" I rein myself in. He's leaving, and he's just trying to make it easier on me. He's excited to leave Shitville because he hates it here, like we all do. He's had his college stuff packed for two weeks.

He's driving fast — something he always does when he's psyched.

"I will wear it," I say, putting it on and loving how thoughtful it is. I will have to put it in a box when he's gone. He and his ballet-teacher mom have loaded up their truck. They are driving cross-country starting at 7:00 A.M. tomorrow.

This hurts so much that I think only the sand in Jamaica could make it better. And only if I swallowed a whole, whole lot of it.

Kevin is clanking beer bottles and whooping around when we arrive.

"You are so lucky, dude," he says, totally out of character, to all of us at the same time. He then goes back into Kevin mode: "I know that alcohol kills brain cells, and I know the dangers of underage beer drinking — like really bad breath. But just for tonight, it is not about what's healthy. Tonight is about us!"

Juliana reaches over and pulls Matt's elbow. "Kiss me!" she says, and he does.

"Woo-hoo!" Cherry jumps up on the couch and does a spread eagle on the way down. I hear her say *ouch* when she lands on Kevin's twenty-pound hand weight.

Frankie tells a joke about a tampon that falls in love with a

Chiclet. Her cousin Eugene somehow got himself invited. They are the oddest couple. He's a conservative Christian and she's a left-wing lesbian allergic to any closet. But they make each other laugh. Under her guidance, he has stopped wearing plaid pants (he wore them without irony). He has also started wearing contacts and stopped talking about the bacteria in his intestines. In a few weeks, he's going to dental school in Florida.

"We're going to show this town what fun is, aren't we, Katie K.?" Cherry whoops while drinking vodka straight out of the bottle. Kevin takes it from her and mixes a drink heavy on the lemonade behind her back. "These losers don't know what they're gonna be missing, do they?"

"They don't." I drop Blue's hand and stand next to Matt. No matter where he goes and no matter how scratchy things are between us, I know he and I will always stay in touch. We are friends. Blue and I are something else.

"Goodness, I wish Juliana would go to Juilliard like she was supposed to," Matt whispers in my ear. She was supposed to study music there, but said she changed her mind so she could be in D.C. with Matt. Even as he whispers this, she's right there on the other side of him. She looks at us suspiciously.

The night goes on, and Blue and I don't say much. The way he holds my hand is enough. He can't stop staring at me. This makes me warm, hot, happy. It also makes me sad.

"You and me," he whispers. "That room over there."

He wants to be alone with me in the toy room that Kevin's little sister, Kelly, outgrew about a year ago. (She is in Florida, thank goodness.) We go in, and there's a red mat on the floor where she used to practice her somersaults. Her dolls are all in a row on a shelf, arranged by height. There are stuffed animals all over. Blue moves them out of the way and moves the mat to the middle of the room.

"I didn't think I could miss someone so much," he says, lying down on it and pulling me with him.

"You're not even gone." I don't let him pull me. It's not that easy.

"Come down here." He is difficult to resist, resting on his elbows, his feet crossed like nothing is changing.

"What's in it for me?"

Then he stands up and kisses me, and I give in. What we do is safe and sweet and special and heartbreaking and electrifying and right but also wrong. Outside I hear rap music, then country, and then they are all yelling because Eugene is doing the Robot to the song "What a Girl Wants."

We are still alone, and we stay alone for a very long time. When our alone is over, there are no words left in my head.

"I love you," I say, looking right at him, and then I want to smack myself with the largest doll on the shelf. I'm not even drunk. I just have no emotional control. I blame it on my hormones, and I curse puberty because I thought it was supposed to give me a break around age eighteen. All I can think is, *Crap, crap, triple crap.*

"Oh my God," he replies. We are still lying down, and he hugs me from behind. He strokes my hand and my hair. He kisses the top of my head. But he still doesn't say a thing. He can't see my face, so he doesn't know that I'm quiet because I'm crying. When I get my eyes back to normal, I gather my clothes and get up.

"I'll miss you." He sits up. "Stay with me, Katie."

I look at him for a long time, not sadly, not sweetly, just looking. Our gaze breaks, and I notice how low the ceiling is in the room and how loud my friends are outside. I need something, but not this.

"You know how I feel," he says, getting up and trying to follow me out to the party as if I'm going back out to the party. "You and me? We just work. But I need more time."

"I know," I answer. All of a sudden, and maybe it's because I have been reading *The Highly Sensitive Person*, I realize that saying "I love you" means all kinds of things — like maybe he shouldn't go so far away to college and maybe we are too young to be so serious and maybe we're just doomed once that word begins its attack on our relationship.

We are out of time. As soon as I get the knot out of the laces of my Skechers, I am walking away. All of a sudden, my emotions stream into one clear thought: *I can hurt now when he is leaving, or I can hurt later when we both realize what I already know* — that long distance plus freshman year just won't work. I don't tell him any of this because I don't want us to say anything hurtful to each other. I want to remember us in the Beetle or on our way to Graceland or giggling about a roll of toilet paper.

"Now I'm going." The Skechers are tied, and I'm standing in the doorway of the toy room looking at him, taking him in for the last time in a long time. "This is a good memory to have, don't you think?"

"Perfect," he answers.

"Please don't call me. Don't text me. I need to not hear from you for four full weeks," I say, and I am not holding back tears, just major emotions that I know I am lucky to have felt.

"Huh?" he asks, reaching for my hand as I pull it away. "But we're not breaking up."

"Yes we are," I say, my eyes firmly holding his. "This is it — officially. We just don't deserve to hurt."

Before he can talk me out of it, I'm gone. I walk out and Kevin gives me a high five because he thinks I just scored in there, which I did, but it's not the happy ending he's imagining. Cherry yells, "Go Hoosiers!" to Kevin even though the school he's going to has the Wildcats for mascots. Frankie gives me a half-smile because she knows what just happened. Matt and Juliana are fighting in the corner. Eugene is picking his nose and wiping it on his pant cuffs and thinks nobody is looking.

I hop in my Beetle and shift into reverse. Someone is fiddling with the driver's-side door handle, and I'm surprised to see it's Matt. "You owe me," he says. So I slow down, let him in, and notice he is smiling. I take off while Blue chases me down Kevin's driveway.

Tears are hot on my cheeks, but I don't feel out of control.

"Thanks, you totally saved me," Matt says, flipping the radio to out-of-character heavy metal. He is tipsy and banging his head. "I did it; I broke it off."

"That's awesome," I say, totally happy for him even if I'm totally sad for myself. I just can't be so vulnerable, sitting in my Shitville room while my boyfriend, now ex, sits in a dorm in San Diego. I'm not mad at him for it. I'm thrilled for him — or at least I will be one day. I have to protect myself in some way because I am so sensitive. If Blue's getting on with his life, I will make choices and get on with mine. Over the song, "Pour Some Sugar on Me," I yell to Matt, "I did, too."

He stops banging and reaches into his pocket, where he still carries a pack of carry-around Kleenexes. He hands me one and says, "I know."

We don't go home because I know that Blue will probably be there waiting for me if I do. I ask Matt to ride with me while I drive to Monmouth Cave. Our plan is to get back after a post-8:00 A.M. Waffle House stop. Blue will be gone by then. On our way, Matt tells me that he's going to Franklin College after all. He is really, really drunk, I realize. This is probably good. He might as well avoid his mom flipping her shit for as long as humanly possible.

Good for him.

I get home, and I only want to sleep. Vicki J. and Bob are sitting right there on the living room couch with a can of Cheeseballs for me.

"Honey, I'm so sorry," Vicki J. says. "I can't tell you he isn't worth it because he is. I can only tell you that your heart is stronger than your stepdaddy's biggest forklift. It really is, honey. It really is."

Bob sighs and hands me an envelope. I go up to my room to open it, and there are two plane tickets to Jamaica. One has my name on it and the other has Cherry's. This is exactly what I need. It leaves at eight that night, and we get to stay at an all-inclusive resort that we are not allowed to leave for one full week. I find out that my mom, Bob, Cherry, Matt, and the rest of my friends have been planning this trip for me all along. These are the best people on the planet, and I feel lucky they care so much about me.

I eat the whole can of Cheeseballs. Then I sleep for four hours. I wake up in my peach room that I'm definitely going to paint yellow as soon as I get back. I rush to pack because I am always running late when it comes to trips.

I hear the doorbell ring, and I'm worried because any visitor is going to make me miss my Jamaica-bound plane.

"Take these with you, mon," Matt says, standing in my bedroom doorway, looking like he's hungover as all of heaven and hell combined. He's shaking all over, and I know it's because he told his parents he was going to Franklin instead of Georgetown. "My dad sat in his chair behind the newspaper, hiding a smile," he tells me.

"What about your mom?" I am trying to pick the sexiest swimsuit I have, which is difficult because they are all one-pieces. I have to go into my mom's room to steal some bikinis as soon as Matt leaves.

"Why do you think I ran out of there and came here?" He sits on the bed, then sees what a rush I'm in and stands back up. "Sorry. Just look in the envelope really quickly," he slurs. I've never seen Matt drink more than one, let alone be this hungover. This is a new era for my reinstated best friend. "You can get into Franklin by winter semester, Katie. You can study psychology. Did you ever think of that? You would be a great therapist."

"Crazy people can't help other crazy people." I am throwing hair products and sunscreen into my suitcase at this point. "But thanks for thinking of me."

"All counselors are especially cuckoo," Matt adds, heading

out the door. "God, I've never met someone who'd be as good at it as you. Um, sorry. Anyway, there's also an application in there for Indiana Southeast — they take open admission until the day classes start September first. I filled them all out for you — essays and everything. You just have to sign and send them as soon as you and Cherry get back."

"I'll think about it," I yell down the hall. He's already at the front door. He is awesome. No one, absolutely no one, knows me as well as he does. "Thank you! Don't let your mom kill you while I'm gone!"

I meet Cherry at the airport, and my mom gives her a lecture about keeping me away from chocolate because I'm deathly allergic to it. Cherry promises, but my mom still looks worried. We head through security alone, and we are giddy about our trip. We are rapping Beastie Boys songs.

At the gate, she puts on red lipstick and tells me there's no way she looks eighteen. Then she adds, "Girl, we are going to have all of the piña coladas you can imagine. Except, do you think they can make them without pineapple? I hate pineapple." At least a week with her will not be emotionally intense, and not thinking is exactly what I need.

We are hula dancing down the aisle of the plane while we look for our seats. I don't know why we're hula-ing in preparation for Jamaica, but it is fun anyway. The overhead speaker reminds us to turn our cell phones off. When I do, I see there's a text message. It's from Blue. My heart does an emergency landing.

*I couldnt wait 4 weeks. 4give me. Have fun n the islands. BTW, Im so n luv witchoo.*

I'm smiling. Really smiling. I turn off my phone and throw it into my backpack. It is resting between the college applications Matt gave me and my next self-help beach read. It's called *Quirkyalone: A Manifesto for Uncompromising Romantics*.

I am ready for liftoff.

# GINGER

## by Christopher Krovatin

I watch the record all day, waiting for him to come and pick it up. And when he does, I am so terrified. It's around 3:45, which is when he usually drops in, when I hear the padding of Converse All-Stars, blue and worn, on the old-fashioned wooden floor. He strolls through calmly, checking out album covers; he is alone this time, unhindered by his obnoxious friends, so he moves fluidly, the musical intake slow and careful. I force myself to look for him over the racks of vinyl discs, and all I can see is the worn-out blue hat on top of a tuft of bright red hair before my nerves shiver and I look back to the order forms I'm sorting. We need three more boxes of the Def Jam Classics lineup, and two more of those Dean Martin records that went so fast. I can almost smell him from here. Oh God. Boy smell. I'm done for.

My eyes go back to the record, the copy of the Dead Kennedys' *Frankenchrist* we got in today. It's an original pressing. On green vinyl. It's pretty rare, according to Popop. There's no way he can afford it. That's not the point, though. Go for the record, Punk Boy. You know you want it.

"Oh, shit . . ." he mumbles, and then crosses over to it and takes it in his hands, scanning the cover, and now I can see him, and he's as stunning as ever. His hair is tousled, sweaty at the tips — it's hot outside, and he's probably just gotten out of a class, like history, or, fingers crossed, a *guitar lesson* — but shining redder than ever under his beaten-and-worn-Holden-Caulfield-fuck-you hat. He wears a blue collared shirt with a white tie and a pair of torn-to-shit jeans that look really, honestly worn down rather than cut up at home in his mom's closet. He moves a bit like a bug, like one who bends and twitches in ways that no one understands but works perfectly. The record comes sliding out of the sleeve and his breath, my breath, catches up in his throat. His green eyes widen, and for a second the green vinyl seems to be the most important thing in the world to him. He scans both sides of the record, spins it in his hands, which move expertly and carefully, which makes me begin to feel just the tiniest bit light-headed.

All I know about him is what I've seen: punk rock, loud friends, a love of irresponsibility. There has to be more there, sadness and poetry and philosophy and an old-school record player at his house, maybe with a Victrola wind-up handle —

"Could I get this?" he asks. I blink, only for a second, and he's at the counter, passing the copy of *Frankenchrist* forward so that I can ring it up, and my palms are sweating, and my neck is too hot, and I need to calm down or else he's going to notice, so I take the record out of his hands and glance at the price tag.

"Forty-five sixty-eight," I say. *Gevalt.*

I can tell by the look on his face that he doesn't have the cash, but he looks in his pockets anyway, as though he might have left a twenty in them when he put the pants in the wash.

He scrambles through all four of his pants pockets, his shirt pocket, and inside every pocket of his wallet before he looks up, defeated, and says, "Ah, crap. I don't have it."

I want to scream and cry and stomp my feet. It's not fair. From the moment I saw that record there, I knew it was his, and now some hipster in flannel is going to grab it before he can. I can see the creep now; he'll stare at the green vinyl as a collector's item, not a jewel; his eyes will swell with greed, not awe, not punk rock *fury*.

I push the record forward. "Take it."

His eyebrows jump. "Sorry?"

OhmyGodohmyGod, what are you doing, Isabel? What are you doing? Tell him it's a joke. Right now.

"Take it," I hear my mouth say. "Quickly. Before my dad gets back here."

"Seriously?"

That's a good question — Are you SERIOUS, Isabel? Popop will be furious. He remembered that record, and he'll notice if the money for it isn't in the register, and you will do more *sweeping* and *filing* than you ever could've imagined. This will come out of your LIFE, young lady.

My head spins. My fingers tingle. I feel decadent and risqué. "Really. Take it. Quickly."

"Uh, I don't know —"

"I've been waiting all day for you to come in and buy it." Oh, wow. I feel like a tightrope walker. Deep breaths. Steady hands. That last comment took you to the Point of No Return. "Take it now. I can't hold on to it for you, and someone who wants it less will get it. Please."

He snatches the record, jumping at my command, and his

81

eyes sparkle at me in exactly the way I thought they would. My blood turns up the flame burning beneath my brain. "Anything I can do for you in return?" he whispers conspiratorially. "I can give you what money I have —"

Well, now, what a question . . .

"Tell me," I say, trying to keep my cool, hoping I'm right about this, "what color your guitar is."

His sparkling smile becomes a grin. "It's green. Like, leprechaun green." At which point he waves, spins on his heel, and scampers out of the door like a little boy, leaving me to bite my lower lip and hope my heart rate slows down for a few seconds.

Green. Of course it is.


My father somehow knows about it, which makes him angry, which makes him a total jerk, which makes him bring it up at the dinner table, which makes Shana drool in sadistic glee.

"You're kidding me," she says in mock excitement. "Our little Isabel did something illegal for some street urchin who hangs around the store? For shame!"

"He's not a street urchin," I mumble between bites of pierogi, "and it's not illegal. It comes out of my pay. I bought it for him."

"Bought, shmought," snaps my dad, pointing his fork at me over his huge beer belly. Popop is the epitome of guy-who-owns-a-record-store: He's a chubby aging Jewish hippie with a huge gray beard and a tendency to overstate ideas. He's brilliant and funny and maybe the nicest man I've ever known, but he's still human, and a rather difficult human at that when it comes to his record collection. "You gave away a limited-edition Dead Kennedys original pressing. To a kid who we know spends money at the store anyway. This is not good business, Izzy."

Shana clucks. "Isabel. Really. Has he even bought you dinner yet?"

My mother, ever the supportive one, looks at me and smiles politely. "Do you know this boy's name, honey?"

"Mom, come on." My sister laughs. "You don't know your crush's name. That's for your imagination later." She winks at me and I want to grab her neck and squeeze and squeeze and *squeeze* . . .

"It's John," I say, looking back to my plate. "I overheard his friends calling him that once or twice. Mostly, they call him 'Irish.'"

"'Irish'?" says my mom, concerned. "Is he a drunkard?"

"Worse, he's a *Ginger*," says my father, chuckling.

"He's really *Irish*?!" Now my mom's really paying attention. "Like, redheaded, pale-and-lanky IRISH boy? Gyah! Izzy, you're killing me."

"Mom, please."

"Can't you have a weird little teenager crush on some nice Jewish boy who comes into the store?" She sighs while Shana cackles. "Why does it have to be the freckled Irishman with the homeless-person clothes?"

If he were here, he'd tell me about his ideas for tattoos. If he were here, he'd write me a punk rock song and wash my family away in a tsunami of distortion.

I'm sweeping the world music aisle when he comes in next, a blazing afternoon about a week after his last visit. My dad's behind the counter, which is troublesome. Even worse — the Ginger Boy has Company with him.

"While I respect your opinions wholeheartedly," says the fat one with the spikes, "anger, when musically expressed, is rarely about tone of voice or general vocal style. In fact, vocals do very little to get across anger. True rage, true *infuriation*, I feel, comes from a general atmosphere given off by the music in question: the tightness of riffs, the emotions invoked by the tone of the bass line, the strength with which the drums are being hit . . . these things release emotion. These things cause understanding of what a song is *about*. So, no matter what lyrics or vocal tones get used, one's music is really what makes a band a happy band or an angry band. Which is why you're absolutely absurd in suggesting that Mindless Self Indulgence is an angrier band than Slayer."

I close my eyes and try to drown it out. More of this talk. Day in, day out at this store, all I hear is this stupid babble. The Ginger Boy doesn't really like having friends like this, I tell myself. They're his stupid sidekicks, the kids he keeps around for laughs.

"While you might be correct on musical atmosphere being the overwhelming factor in categorizing a band," says the skinny one with all the hair and the nice clothes, "you have to take attitude and subject matter into account, both of which are displayed primarily through the lyrics of songs. When you look at, say, a Nick Cave song, you can determine whether or not the tone will be overwhelmingly sad or happy or angry through the first couple of notes, but with certain songs — for example, 'The Curse of Milhaven' — one discovers a song which is even more angry or miserable due to the fact that the atmosphere

84

presents itself as one of happiness and fun while the lyrics are drenched in woe. It taints that innocence and reckless joy by defining the song with a trait not normally assigned to this atmosphere or music. So Slayer sounds like the kind of music a Satanist listens to — what of it? The songs are about serial killers, battlefields, and hell. It's expected that they're angry. Mindless Self Indulgence, on the other hand, sing about gay sex and cocaine over happy, punky, industrial pop — they're the kind of music that the hopped-up guy at the gas station around three in the morning listens to, and that pink-haired, tattooed, burrito-sucking, methed-out motherfucker is one ANGRY kid. Therefore, their anger is more apparent, and therefore I believe them to be the angrier band."

"Can I help you boys?" asks my father, looking up from his copy of *Rolling Stone*.

"Nah, we're just browsing, thanks."

"Okay, well . . ." He looks at me warily, then back at the boys. "Just let me know if you need any help looking for anything."

"Thanks, man," the spiked one continues. "Brent, you're full of it. I know it's hard to believe, but you're just full of it. Your argument doubles back on you and kicks you in the ass. What you're saying to me is that atmosphere in music can be enhanced by mismatching the lyrical content and lyrical tone of a song, making a song seem . . . asymmetrical, as it were. This works, I suppose, in that it upsets the listener's perception of normal music and therefore enhances certain characteristics of that type of song. While this makes MSI a *scary* band, I certainly don't think it makes them an *angry* band. My argument was that atmosphere is displayed first and foremost by the music, that lyrics are and should be only accompaniment on top of music, poetry that elaborates on the general tone of a song. Therefore, when those lyrics are mismatched to that tone, they go against the song as a whole and the listener ends up just taking the song less seriously. In short: While your idea is interesting, it isn't a valid detractor from mine. Slayer are angry overwhelmingly; everything about their music drips pure, unfiltered rage. MSI have a certain fury to them, but their music smacks of sarcasm, leaving little to no room for serious consideration in the realms of musical categorization. Saying that MSI are angrier than Slayer is saying that expressing something honestly does less than when one is expressing it ironically, which, no offense, I just can't believe. I *won't* believe. The kid at the gas station IS very angry, yes. 'Cause he's a BITCH, and he's bored out of his stupid-ass skull with his stupid-ass life."

"That's touching, Conan."

"I know, I'm like your fucking shrink or something. Found anything yet, Irish?"

I hear a rack full of records sliding backward, and then his voice — his graveled, world-worn voice — calls out, "Excuse me?"

"Yes?" asks my father, sounding a little annoyed.

"Is the girl who works here around?"

My heart leaps into my throat and immediately stops beating.

"You mean Isabel? My daughter?" I can hear the immediate disapproval in Popop's voice. He can see me, though the Ginger Boy can't; the counter is sort of the center of everything in the store, staring out across all of the aisles. But Popop doesn't even look my way, just keeps staring at the boy, his eyes narrow.

86

"I think so, yeah," John says. "Skinny girl, straight brown hair?"

Popop looks at me, and I can see he's leaving the choice up to me. I stare at the floor instead of responding. I have no idea what to do in this situation. How to handle it. What can he possibly have to say to me? Finally my father takes the neutral route. "Isabel, honey? You around?"

I stay silent for a couple of seconds, and then I grip the broom, stand up straight, and say, "I'm over here." He motions with his head, and I hear footsteps approach my aisle. Do something, Izzy. Sweep. Rearrange records. Don't just stand here like a guilty prisoner. What'll he say if he knew that you turned to stone the minute he spoke? What kind of girlfriend would that make —

He turns the corner, and he's there, all round-faced and freckled, his cap looking even more antique and beautiful than ever.

"Hey," he says, reaching out his hand, "I'm John."

"Isabel," I say, and shake it carefully. His hands are warm and smooth. Mine are probably clammy and sickly. I want to immediately say something about how I don't see a lot of sunlight, but shutting up works, too.

"I wanted to, eh . . ." He looks down at his Converses, then back at me. "I just wanted to thank you for giving me that record. It was really cool of you to hold on to it for me until you saw me. It's a great album. And the question about my guitar was pretty awesome, too."

I nod and say, "No problem." Then, out of nowhere, I spew out, "I mean, I've noticed you around."

He smiles. "Uh-oh. I'm being watched."

"No, it's not like that. I mean, it is, in that, like, I've been watching you when you've come around the store, and I've seen what kind of records you like, so I know what you'd probably want to buy when you come in here next, but that's it, it's not, like, creepy or worried or anything, I just watched you around because you have really specific tastes and 'cause your hair is so bright red. You're noticeable. Watchable."

*Gevalt*, Izzy. What have you done?

He stares at me for a bit. His eyes are wide, his mouth hanging open. He pushes his hands into his pockets and tries to talk, but finally comes out with, "When do you get off work?"

*GEVALT*, Izzy. What have you *done*?!

"Uh, at five. But I have a paper to write tonight."

"What kind of paper?"

"Uh, poetry. Milton. He wrote *Para* —"

"I actually read a lot of Milton. Any chance we could get some coffee after you get off and talk about Milton a bit?"

This must be what getting high is like. Like being on another planet. Like the best song you've ever heard, only a million times stronger and more poetically right. The planets align. I can barely move. "I'll have to check with my father, but I'd really . . . yeah. That'd be great."

"Okay, well," he says, "I guess I'll come by here at five then."

"Okay."

"Well."

"Yeah."

"I guess I should, uh —"

Suddenly two heads appear over his shoulders, both leering giddily at me.

"We understand you like our friend very much," says the

88

skinny one, "but we feel it's our duty to tell you that he's been convicted of sodomy in three different states."

"With *bunny rabbits*."

"Right, exactly. He sodomizes bunny rabbits all the time. We thought you should know."

"We're just that fucking good to people who like our friends."

"Our honesty knows no bounds."

"We're like Santa Claus. Jesus, even."

"It's hard, being the bearer of bad news."

"Bunny-sodomizing news, especially."

"It's a dirty job, but some—"

"All right, guys, you made your fucking point," he says, brushing them away from his shoulders while his freckles blend in crimsonly with the rest of his face. I feel my own cheeks burst into flames. Looking back to me, his eyes are pleading, scream-ing, *Please, please, please excuse my idiot friends*. He tries to smile it off, but he's wavering. It's adorable. "Five-ish? I'll be outside?"

I nod a little too hard, saying, "Yup."

"Okay. Well . . . later."

*LATER. Oh my GOD*. "'Bye."

"Brent, do me a favor?"

"Yeah?"

"Here're a couple bucks. When you see your mom later, will you give them to her?"

"Wow, couldn't see that one coming, guys."

"Hey, sodomizer, no one asked for your fucking opinion. Should I be listening to the Descendents, by the way? They seem good, but are they worth buying?"

"Yeah, totally, they're awesome."

"Fabulous. Let's hit the weed spot."

The bell on the door jangles, and they're gone, cackling their way down the street toward St. Mark's, leaving me to my disapproving father and more huddled sweeping.

"You are not going out with this boy, Isabel," says my dad into his magazine.

"It'll just be coffee, Dad. He's going to help me with my paper."

"I know boys like that, Izzy. They don't want to help you with any papers or anything. They're interested in just one thing. And you know what that is?"

*Me*, I think as my head bobs airily at the end of its string. *Me me me.*


The next thing I know, my head is in a blue haze of cigarette smoke and I'm clutching a cup of coffee that's far too big for my hands or anyone's. The table we're at is wooden, old, covered in graffiti, and sloppily carved with love/hate declarations. All around us are punks and mods and misfits and street rats, their glittering jewelry and piercings and colorful hair blending almost seamlessly into the stained-glass mosaic walls. He's sipping at a Coke, flipping through a worn paperback of *Paradise Lost*. He looks wary. I find that hilarious. Not in a laughing way, though.

"So, I was thinking we'd talk about the introduction first," he says, glancing at his note-covered copy, "and then go through the twelve arch-demons, explain their history, their importance."

"Okay."

"Most of them are ancient gods, y'know. Milton just had to make 'em demons to explain to the church that writing a huge-ass poem about Satan was actually a Christian endeavor rather than just a fucked-up artistic vision."

"Right."

He looks at the book again and then tosses it haphazardly onto the table. "Why'd you ask me the question about my guitar?"

Every muscle in my body tenses up at once. A shiver runs through the tip of my fingers and courses its way down into my ribs and jaw, but I dare not move, just in case my entire body would fall apart and clatter loudly to the floor. "Uh, sorry?"

"Why'd you ask me the question about my guitar?"

"I, uh, just thought . . ." Come ON, Isabel, you're blowing this. Just open your mouth and talk. There's a perfectly good answer to this question. "There's, uh, I didn't mean, it wasn't, I, uh —"

"It's 'cause I'm the Redheaded Punk Kid, right?" He says it staring straight into my eyes, a stern look on his face.

Izzy, he's found you out. You're finished. All the cute little teenage-girl thoughts that have been running through your weird little mind for the past couple of months every time you see him have been blatantly obvious, and tonight you've been made the fool. He's been humoring your nonsense for a while; he's been making you feel wanted and pretty so that you won't be as terrified of him. Good job. You're officially a grade-A chump. Abort. Abort.

"Yeah," I finally manage to get out, and start getting ready to go. "That's exactly it. Sorry."

"You're leaving?"

Now I'm angry; I can't help it. Before, it was sweet, in a way. Now, it's just cruel. "Yes, I'm leaving," I say decisively. "Of course I'm leaving. Why would you want to sit here with me after you've just said that, and I've just admitted it? What's the fucking point?" Wow. I don't usually talk like this. I feel my face burn. God, when can this stop? "You're the Redheaded Punk Kid. You're so handsome, and crazy, and a little too rebellious for your own good. What the hell am I supposed to be?"

He stands up, pushing his chair away, a little smile creeping along his face. "You're the Beautiful Girl From the Record Store."

What?

"What?"

"It's okay," he says, reaching out a hand as if to ease me back in my chair. "It's okay that I'm the Redheaded Punk Kid. I got that. It's all good. Because you're the Beautiful Girl From the Record Store. I know exactly what you're thinking. I've been following this train of thought for a while. You can relax. It's actually appropriate."

I'm shaking. I almost feel like crying, though I'm not sure why. "So, what . . . what does this mean? If anything? Because I would really, really like —"

"It means I want to kiss you," he says, "because the Redheaded Punk Kid is always totally falling for the Beautiful Girl From the Record Store."

"So this is, what? Routine?" I laugh harshly. "Tradition?"

"More of a *confession*," he says.

Fire and music, all through my brain. Angelic throngs and booming trumpets. There was no better answer to that question than the one he just gave. Circumstance was truly smiling upon me. "So. Wow. Um." Izzy. Wake up. "I should go. I'm sorry. I need to —"

"Here," he says, putting up his hands. "Okay. That was a bit much at once, right?"

"Right."

"Well, here. I'll see you at the store tomorrow. I'll stop by. And we'll talk."

"I'm sorry. I want to stay, I just — I'm really . . ." Ugh. I can feel my throat, my eyes, tighten up and wring out. Calm DOWN. "I'm just really shy." I hold my Milton to my chest like a life preserver. "And this is new. And I'm worried. But this, I —"

"No, it's cool."

"I'm sorry."

"No worries. I'll see you tomorrow."

"Right. 'Bye."

And then I'm rushing out in the cool night air, letting the heat waft off me and hoping I can start breathing again soon.

When I come out of the back room the next day, he's there, but so is my sister. They're leaning against the used rock T to W racks, him looking amused and casual, her on display, showing him what he's missing by not being curled up in a sleeping bag somewhere with her. Her clothes, her facial expression, the predatory gleam in her eyes, it all screams, *This one is mine, oh, so mine.* I hate her more than anything right now. She never even saw him before today, but she knows, she knows it's my boy, and she wants him for no other reason than that. I step back a bit and listen to them.

"So, that cap looks like it's seen better days."

"Yeah, it's my bad-luck cap. I wear it everywhere."

"It's cool. It has sort of punk rock thing to it."

"Yeah, well, I'm into punk rock." You twit, Shana. You can see that just looking at him. Maybe if you knew about him, or his music, or RECORDS, you could figure that out on your own.

"I see you around the store a lot."

"Really? I've gotten that before."

"Yeah. You're jogging through with those two other kids. Y'know."

"My boys, right. I dunno — we all love this place. I really just come for the girl, though, y'know?"

My heart seizes up. Shana laughs like Cruella de Vil. "The 'girl'?"

"Yeah, Isabel? She works here. Do you know her?"

"Izzy's my sister! Why on *earth* do you come around here to see her?"

"Ooooh! *You're* the Trashy Sister."

"Pardon?!"

"Y'see, Isabel's the Beautiful Girl From the Record Store. And every Beautiful Girl From the Record Store has a Trashy Sister who's kind of a bitch. Sometimes, they're sisters-in-law. Huh. Now that I look at you, it makes perfect sense. You sort of look like her. Only, y'know . . . trashy."

"Wow. That's real sweet, asshole."

"Sorry, Trash. Wish I could help."

"Go fuck yourself, you piece of delinquent shit. My father will know about this. You'll never be able to come in here again." She stalks off, his childish laughter following her. The bell jingles, and she's gone, off down the street in a huff of swear-words and flipped hair.

I step out from behind the door to the back room and stare at my Venus in Converse.

"Hi," I say.

He looks up, startled, and smiles. "Well, hey."

"Can I help you?"

"I certainly hope so."

# HALFWAY

### by Coe Booth

I know I ain't s'posed to be driving by myself with nothing but a hour-old permit in my back pocket, but a brotha got places to go. Alright, to be honest, I don't got nowhere to go, but this dude from my old building was dumb enough to lend me his car to go to the Motor Vehicles, so why not cruise 'round for a while?

I had to take the permit test twice before I passed it, but I ain't study or nothing, so I can't complain. Most of them questions was just common sense, you ask me, 'cept for them ones 'bout blood-alcohol levels and how many feet you gotta park behind a fire hydrant and shit. But all that matter now is, the permit got my name on it and a fucked-up picture of me, so I'm good to go. Only thing, if I get pulled over by the police, they gonna probably arrest my black ass for not having no licensed driver in the car with me, but I'm trying not to think 'bout that right now. I mean, it's my birthday. Sixteen fuckin' years old. I gotta do something 'til tonight.

'Bout midnight me and my friends is gonna get together to go out partying and, knowing them dudes, it's gonna be going down all weekend. That's the good thing 'bout having a birthday on a Friday. The party don't gotta stop 'cause nobody got nothin' to do the next day.

But for now I'm cruisin'. Got the radio on, loud, and the windows is down 'cause, even though it's the end of March, it feel like it's summer today. And the girls is out showing off they skin already. So what the fuck else I'ma do? Sit in that hot-ass apartment by myself? Hell no. Nothing wrong with blasting my music and checking out the best the Bronx got to offer.

I'm on East Tremont, and it's busy today. Folks must got money 'cause they shopping, walking 'round with all kinda bags and shit. But it's the girls I'm watching. They got all kinda females in this part of town. There's the 'round-the-way girls, the kind with the tight jeans, sneakers, and tank tops with the bra straps showing. They the kind that can look good even when they rockin' baseball caps or scarfs on they head. And they the kinda girls you can just chill with 'cause they grew up in your same neighborhood and you been knowing them forever. They cool.

And there's the good girls with the Catholic school uniforms, the real short kind with the white socks and shit. They hot, but don't hardly know it yet. And you wanna be there when they find out.

And, course, there's the ghetto girls. They the kind that be walking 'round with nothing but fake name-brand clothes, the kind you get from them Senegalese dudes on Amsterdam Avenue in Harlem. One day they be wearing fake Gucci everything, from the jacket to the T-shirt to the jeans to the sneakers to the backpack. Then the next day they be all in fake Fendi. They the girls that be wearing them big gold earrings, got weaves down they back, and them long fake nails with the designs and shit on them. They the kinda girl you gotta work to get. 'Cause they ain't gonna want no broke nigga like me.

I keep driving, working my way over by Westchester Square. I'm trying to see everything going on, but keep my eyes on the road at the same time. Funny thing is, I can't drive for shit. Straight up. Them people that gave me this permit musta been out they mind 'cause I don't need to be out here. 'Specially by myself. But I ain't had no choice. I ain't had nobody to show me how to drive.

That was s'posed to be my pops job. Man, we talked 'bout that for a while, 'bout how he was gonna give me lessons and shit. Matter of fact, he let me drive 'round some parking lots a couple times just for practice. Shit was funny, too. He was always thinking I was gonna crash, like I wasn't looking where I was going. Like I wasn't listening to what he was trying to teach me.

But them real driving lessons never happened 'cause my pops got locked up in September. Just like that. And now that I'm old enough to learn how to drive for real, on the streets and shit, he gone. So when it come to learning how to drive, it look like that's just another thing I'ma hafta figure out on my own.

And I gotta admit, I'm driving mad crazy. I swear. Every time I see a hot girl, I steer the car in her direction without even thinking 'bout what I'm doing. I can't help it. And I run through a couple red lights like there ain't no other cars out here. Folks is hittin' they horns and probably cursing me out, but I don't care. I'm liking what I see.

When I finally do stop at a red light, two white girls cross the street in front of my car. They look alright, too. They both

98

got on short jackets, jeans, and heels, and both of them is skinny but not all bony and shit. They working what they got.

Now, me myself, I'm into the sistahs, but I wouldn't be normal if I ain't check these girls out. A man gotta look. Only thing, while I'm looking, one of them turn her head and look at me. She talking to her friend and smiling, and when she see me she keep on smiling. And she don't turn away from me, neither. She keep her eyes on mines. Damn.

I'm thinking 'bout saying something to her, but I don't know what kinda line white girls wanna hear. And I think 'bout the jacked-up hooptie I'm in, and I don't know if them girls is gonna wanna be seen talking to a dude with this kinda car. And the car ain't even mines.

But I check myself out in the rearview mirror anyway, and I'm looking good as usual, so I'm just 'bout to make my move and yell something out the window when the light change and them horns start going again. Assholes. Like they can't wait a minute. Like they in a rush to get to the next fuckin' light. The girls run to the curb before they get run over, laughing the whole time, and I don't got no choice 'cept to take my eyes off them and keep driving down the street. And that's probably the one fucked-up thing 'bout driving. You gotta keep going in the same direction 'cause them other folks ain't gonna let you just stop in the middle of the street to talk to no female. And I never made no U-turn in my life, and I ain't 'bout to try one now.

When I get to Westchester Square, I see a McDonald's and I'm like, yeah, it's my birthday. I'ma get me a Quarter Pounder. With cheese. And I'ma go through the drive-thru 'cause I got a car now and ain't nothing better than eating in the car.

Now, I been through a drive-thru like a million times, but I wasn't never behind the wheel before. And, straight up, it's a whole 'notha thing when you the one driving. Not only do you gotta think 'bout how to drive, you gotta think 'bout what you wanna order, and where you s'posed to order from. You gotta turn your music down, order, get your money ready, pay the kid, then pull the car up to the next window, and then they finally give you your food. Ain't nothing easy 'bout none of it. But after a lot of hittin' the brakes and movin' forward, I make it happen.

A couple minutes later, I'm eatin' and cruisin' down Westchester Avenue. Got my food in one hand and it's a mess with the lettuce and ketchup and shit spilling all over the place. And now I'm driving with only one hand, like I got it like that.

But, to be honest, I still ain't got nowhere to go. I ain't ready to go back to the projects and give the car up. Not yet. It's something after five o'clock, and I can't be driving 'round all day doing nothing. Truth is, it's nice being on my own, independent, doing what I wanna do. That's the best thing 'bout driving. Behind the wheel, it's like you know you in control 'cause you can feel it. You free.

Freedom.

Man, freedom ain't nothing to mess with. I should know. Not that I ever been locked up or nothing, but my pops, he would still be locked up now if he wasn't transferred from Rikers to some kinda halfway house in Queens last week. Some kinda place where they put convicts 'til they sentence is up. My pops friend Regg told me where the place is at, and told me I should go visit the man. But I was like, I got better things to do. I'm not gonna see him 'til he back home. Which is where he shoulda kept his ass in the first place.

Now, in the car with no place to go really, I'm thinking maybe I will go to that halfway house. But not to hang out and chill. Nah. If I roll up there, I'ma do it to let my pops know how much he fucked up. I been keeping a lot of shit inside, and I'm tired of it. I know I'm only sixteen and he gonna tell me I ain't no man yet, but 'cause of him, I'm grown. 'Cause of him, I had to try and hold shit together while he was sitting on his ass in jail. And he need to know that.

And there's shit I need to know my damn self. Like why a grown man can't keep hisself home with his family. Like why he be going 'round talking 'bout how much he love us but don't never stop doing all that illegal shit he know gonna get him arrested. That ain't right.

Now, most of the time, I don't be walking 'round mad 'bout what my pops do or don't do. Least I don't be showing it to no one. 'Cause he his own man. And if he wanna sell drugs, he gonna do it whether he need to or not. Whether it jack us up or not. But I ain't feeling the same no more. Today, I got things to say.

Before I know it, I'm on the Cross Bronx, on my way to the Whitestone Bridge. To Queens. I ain't really thinking what I'm doing. I'm just keeping my eyes on the road, trying to follow the signs. And when I get near the tollbooth, I try to work myself into the right lane, the one that take money, 'cause I don't got no kinda E-ZPass. I gotta turn my music down just to concentrate on counting the money out and handing it to the man in the booth. And, damn, a police car pull up in the E-ZPass lane next to mines and I don't wanna do nothing to look guilty, so I pull off mad smooth, cool. Like I be driving every day. And the cops pull off, too, and for a while they driving right next to me, but it don't look like they paying me no mind. By the time I'm

101

actually on the bridge, I see them pull ahead of me, and they gone. And I don't know what I was sweating for.

Driving 'cross bridges is scary as hell with all them metal grooves and shit. They got my car moving all over the place, and I gotta hold the wheel real tight to keep the car under control. And at the same time, I'm looking down off the bridge and out to all them buildings and trees and shit on the other side of the water and, with the sun going down, everything look real nice. I'm not sure if I'm looking at Queens or Manhattan or even New Jersey, but wherever that is over there look like a place I wanna check out one day.

I hold the wheel tighter and concentrate on what I'm doing again. One crazy move to the right and I'm in the fucking water, and to the left, I'ma be in the side of some other car. I can't make no mistakes. I hope everyone else out here know how to drive 'cause I don't want them fucking me up, neither. It's like when you driving you gotta trust people, and I don't hardly trust nobody.

But, for real, this is nice, driving. Ain't nothing like this feeling. Not even the best weed make me feel this good. It's like I got power or something. I can do what I want in this car. And I know it's gonna be mad hard to go back to taking the train again 'cause I can get used to this.

The second I'm over the bridge, it hit me. I don't know shit 'bout Queens. Yeah, I know the halfway house address, and I know it's in Hollis over by where my pops used to go to buy all his DJ equipment and records, but I don't know how to get there from here. The cars on the highway is flying and all I'm trying to do is stay in my lane. I'm only doing 'bout sixty, but still, all the other cars is going 'round me and shit. Making me feel like a chump or something. I'm passing LaGuardia Airport and, man, I ain't even know it was so close to the Bronx. Truth is, I ain't never been to no airport before.

I start picking up speed, 'cause I'm staying in the lane real good now, 'specially since there ain't no girls out there to turn my head. But in the back of my mind I still don't know why I'm even speeding, 'cause I don't know how to get to 220th Street anyway, and when I get there what I'ma do? Look my pops in the face and just curse him out?

Not that I'm scared to do that, 'cause I ain't. For real. I got a lot of shit to tell him, and a lot of what I hafta say gonna hurt him.

And what the fuck is a halfway house anyway? Halfway to what? Halfway to being free? 'Cause only thing my pops is halfway to is halfway back to his fucked-up family. Halfway back to a family that had to live in a shelter while he was chillin' behind bars. All 'cause he had to take one of them vacations that he find a way to take every couple years so he can forget his responsibilities for a while. I mean, I'm like this: If the man needed to get away from us, he coulda got on one of them planes at LaGuardia and went to some island or something. 'Cause it woulda been the same fucking thing, far as I'm concerned.

Halfway house. I don't even know what to expect when I find the place. I mean, it ain't no jail, so is there gonna be a fence and barbed wired and shit 'round the house? Is there gonna be, like, correction officers there or just some kinda security guards? I mean, somebody gotta be there to make sure them dudes don't just up and leave. Regg told me the halfway house is only for nonviolent offenders, so they probably don't need no armed guards watching them niggas. They ain't no threat to nobody. Not really. I mean, my pops wasn't doing nothing a lot of folks don't be doing on a regular basis. He just dumb enough to keep getting hisself caught.

It don't matter no way. Whatever the place is like or who they got guarding them dudes, I don't care. I'm just gonna roll up there, park the car right in front, and ring the bell. And when my pops come to the door, the first thing he gonna ask me is how I got out there, and I'ma shake the keys in his face and point to the car like it's mines and be like, "You don't see my ride?" And I'ma smile and tell him 'bout how I be going wherever I want now. By myself. And how I don't need nobody to take me nowhere 'cause I'm my own man now.

That's how our conversation gonna start. I ain't gonna give him no time to say nothing, neither. I'ma be the one doing all the talking. And when I'm through, he gonna know why I drove all the way out to Queens to see his ass. He gonna know I'm for real.

And I can just see his face while I'm telling him all this shit. First he gonna be surprised, 'cause I ain't never got in my pops face before. Me, I always had mad respect for the man. But that respect been gone. And he gonna know that. Feel that. Then, when he see that I'm not backing down from him, he gonna get mad. 'Cause when a man fuck up, he don't wanna hear 'bout it from his kid. But it don't matter what he say or what he do. All I want is for him to stand there and listen.

I pass Shea Stadium, another place I ain't know was so close. But baseball ain't never been my thing really. Not my pops thing, neither. The only time I ever been to a baseball game was when my school took us to Yankee Stadium when I was in, like, third grade or something. Only thing I remember was the Yankees lost, and this girl Kenya started crying. Man, she ain't never heard the end of that shit. Never.

I drive a couple more minutes, but I know I gotta get off the highway anyway and see what the street numbers is. Then I can try to get to 220th through the streets. It's gonna take longer, but I ain't in no rush.

I get in the right lane and get off at the next exit. I'm just 'bout to start looking for some street signs with numbers on them when my cell ring. It's on the front seat in my backpack, so I'm digging for it with my right hand and steering with my left, which ain't easy. Least not for me. Not yet. Good thing there ain't a whole lot of cars out here right now 'cause I ain't driving all that straight no more.

I can't look at the caller ID while I'm driving 'cause I don't got them kinda skills, so I just flip the cell open and go, "What up?"

"Ty, where you at, man?"

It's Ray, the guy that own this piece of car.

"Cruisin'," I tell him.

"You ain't fucking up my car or nothing, right?"

"Nah, I can drive, man."

"Yeah, right. I seen how you pulled out the projects a couple hours ago. You almost hit two parked cars, and you damn near ran over Ms. Lucas from Building D."

We both start laughing. "She old, anyway," I say. "Lady on borrowed time now."

"You stupid, man," he say, still laughing. "When you coming back with my ride?"

"When you need it?"

"I'm good, man. Chillin' with my girl 'til your party start. I was just, you know, making sure I still got a car, 'cause, man, you one non-drivin' nigga."

I don't tell him that I drove on the highway and over the Whitestone Bridge by myself 'cause he probably ain't gonna wanna hear none of that. "I'ma bring your car back, man," I tell him.

"Alright," he say. "It's your birthday. You can hang. Just don't bring my car back with no empty tank." He hang up, and I flip the cell closed. Then I look down at the dashboard and it's just 'bout on E. The fuel light is on and everything, and I ain't even notice it.

Shit. I gotta find me a gas station. Maybe by then I can figure out where the hell I'm at. I drive 'bout ten, twelve blocks before I see a station and I pull up at the pump like ain't nothin' but a thing, like I be doing this all the time. I cut the engine, get out, and I'm 'bout to go in to pay for my gas when this white dude at the pump 'cross from mines point to my car. I'm like, "What?"

"Your tank," he say. "It's on the other side."

Damn. That's some embarrassing shit. "Thanks," I say. "It's my friend car."

He laugh a little. "Everybody does that. I had this car for four years. No, five. And my wife, she still doesn't know which side our tank is on."

"She pro'ly just doing that so you keep filling it up."

He laugh again. "You're probably right."

He seem like he okay, so before I even think 'bout it good, I ask him, "You know where Two-hundred-twentieth Street is at?"

"Two-hundred-twentieth? You have a ways to go." Then he try to explain that I'm in Flushing, and Hollis is all the way on the other side of Queens. He give me directions to get to Jamaica Avenue and tell me if I stay on that I'ma get where I'm going. I thank the guy, get back in the car, and turn it 'round. Then I go into the store and give up my last nine dollars for gas. Shit.

I pumped gas a couple times for my pops, so that ain't no problem. And it only take a minute to put nine dollars worth of gas in a car. Man, them numbers on that meter is flying. I'm just hoping it's enough to get me where I'm going and back 'cause, if it ain't, I'ma be walking back to the Bronx then. I start the car and can't hardly see the dashboard no more, not 'til I put the headlights on, and when I do, I see that the gas ain't really do shit 'cause I still don't even got a quarter tank. Then to make things worse, I get mad lost trying to find Jamaica Avenue. For a while I think that white guy probably ain't gave me the right directions, but then I find the place he told me to turn at, and Jamaica is right there. Now I just gotta go straight. The street numbers is going up, but I ain't nowhere near 220th Street. And to be honest, that's good 'cause I need the time. To think.

My music is blastin', but I ain't hardly hearing it really. My mind is at that fuckin' halfway house and what's gonna happen when I show up there. I mean, what I'ma do when I see my pops face-to-face? I ain't seen him in months, and yeah, I'm pissed at him, but I know the second he see me standing there, he gonna smile and try to hug me or something. And what I'ma do then? Push the man away? Tell him to go fuck hisself? I don't know.

Jamaica Avenue is busy tonight, but we still moving kinda

107

fast. Matter of fact, it's kinda crazy out here. Dudes on bikes is weaving in and outta traffic like they trying to get killed or something, and cabs is just pulling over and stopping to pick people up like they the only cars out here. And me, I'm just keeping my eyes on them street numbers: 99, 100, 101, and all of a sudden, Hollis, Queens don't seem all that far away no more.

And even though there ain't nothin' but females up and down the street, I'm only half noticing them. I mean, I see them, yeah, but I can't even let my mind go there. 'Cause I'm getting closer now. And looking at girls is cool and everything, but I can't do that all the time.

I stop at a red light and turn the music off so I can think. It ain't the driving I worrying 'bout now. Nah. I'm thinking 'bout who I'm driving to and what's gonna happen when I get out there. 'Cause, the thing is, my pops, he real cool. He ain't gonna ask me why I ain't come out to Rikers to see him all that time. And he ain't gonna hold nothing against me, neither. He gonna be happy to see me. And, to be honest, I don't know if I'ma be able to stay mad at him. Not right then when I see him. 'Cause it's been a while.

And I know him. He definitely gonna remember it's my birthday and he gonna be all happy that I came all the way out here to spend my birthday with him. He gonna tell me that when he get out, me and him gonna really celebrate the way we did last year. 'Cause that was a wild night. First, I hung out with my boys at some dude apartment in Harlem. Then, at 'bout four in the morning, I met up with my pops at this club he was DJing at and, when he was through, me and him got stupid drunk together. Man, I don't even remember how we got home.

But that was last year, and shit ain't the same. And I gotta keep that in mind. 'Cause the second I let him hug me, that's gonna be it. Next thing I know, we gonna be talking and he gonna be making me laugh, telling me 'bout all kinda crazy shit that happened when he was in prison, and after all that, I ain't gonna be able to tell him what I'm planning to tell him. 'Cause all them feelings I got in me now is gonna settle back down again. And there ain't never gonna be no other chance to tell him. Me and him is just gonna go back to the way we was before. We gonna be cool with each other. Tight. We gonna act like nothing never happened 'cause that's the way we always do. 'Til the next time he fuck up.

And I'm like this: I ain't going through none of that no more. I ain't gonna let my pops slide again. 'Cause then he only gonna keep doing the same stupid shit he always do. And I don't need it. I'm free of him.

I pull the car over at the next corner, 110th Street, and wait 'til the street clear up a little bit. Then I make a real fucked-up U-turn, the first one I ever make, and go back the way I came from. Back to the Bronx.

I put my music back on, real loud again, and try not to think 'bout nothing. Not now. Shit. My pops ain't going nowhere 'til August. It's my fuckin' birthday. Why I gotta drive all the way to Hollis tonight?

# EIGHT MINUTES

## by Tanuja Desai Hidier

In her dream, the boy is walking the thin, tight edge of fence. In his hand, swaying — a stick of fluted wood. His features are effaced by a brilliant wash of mango light in the slow pulsing night; from his head spring curls like the stretching limbs of undersea plants. He is very small. In dreams she has seen him, but today knows who he is when through a window thrown open he sings a song of longing to the moon. He sings, in a voice tremulous as a day beginning, of how the moon is desire; it folds seas into tides and girls into women, it tugs with a childish persistence at all the spinning blue earth it would clasp if it could. But the moon is desire without means; it is not powerful enough to gather the Earth to its cratered heart, nor so intrepid to venture closer. Instead, it circles its great love slowly, continually held at arm's length. In her dream she remembers herself, and is overcome with a great and strange sorrow, for now she knows this: The moon is a broken heart that is not real, and it has the face of the boy.

As she floats slowly upward out of this vision, she realizes she must have dozed off. Dreaming, it seemed much longer, but the clock over the television screen upon which the talk show host is dropping his mouth open in utter amazement reads 5:52. The clock is next to the sandalwood frame strung with fake ruby prayer beads, which captures a moment in time she longs for and cannot bear to look upon: her daughter's sixteenth birthday. Upstairs, the girl's bedroom is empty; she has not been sixteen for two years now, and has not been home in nearly one. Each minute of that year, the woman thinks, has curved into the tide that pulls the girl away, further still.

Her lap is white with the handkerchiefs she has been folding since four o'clock; they are soft and forgotten like love letters left in the rain. She knows she will be receiving her daughter's call soon, with the grace of the gods before her husband's impending arrival.

—Please, Kayla, tell me once it's done, she said last night, her hand gripping the receiver till it throbbed.

—Oh, Mummy, what's the point? the girl said. —How can it matter anymore?

—I don't ask for much, Kayla. Please. Do that for me.

She was dozing and now her braid of silvering hair is loose and the scent of distant places travels languorously to her from the incense sticks burning to their ends in the temple in the other room. The temple used to be a kitchen cupboard until its doors were stripped from their hinges and hibiscus petals the shade of late blood and stout yellow candles and a brass incense holder were placed round a Krishna of filigreed ivory to replace the blender and electric can opener, the cans of condensed milk it opened, whirring. In Krishna's hands is a flute.

She stood at the temple at seven o'clock that morning as she did every morning, the gravel scattering icily in the drive as her husband pulled out and headed to the hospital to begin rounds. She clasped her hands together and pressed them to her lips, her seven bangles glinting a frenetic melody down her forearm. She lowered her head and closed her eyes but could still see, her lids vesseling blue, could still feel the knowledge beating in her wrists, throat's hollow, and in the arcs of fatigue round her eyes: that, three hours later, at *her* seven o'clock, the girl would be waking in the two-bedroom walk-up apartment after a night of not sleeping on her faded pull-out couch, stumble into the kitchen, a desert wanderer granted neither food nor drink, but not desiring them anyway, and would, later, not even be able to draw the dusky curve of kohl across her upper lids as she had every morning since the age of twelve; makeup significantly increased the risk of contamination during the procedure. She would sit at her table and regard the vanishing moon from the window and wait for him to wake up or pick her up or whatever had been decided.

—He'll take care of me, Mummy, the girl assured her on the telephone the night before.

—But he didn't take care of you.

—I keep telling you. It was nobody's fault.

—No, she said quietly. —It might have been your fault, but now it's simply your fate.

The girl sighed, a sigh from California which came in through the kitchen window across the country at which the woman stood, as a wind wet with rain. The girl was silent and the woman knew they were both crying.

In her lap float layers of white handkerchiefs. She fills her mind with the image of them until there is only white. The ice clinks, forming in the freezer. The pipes tap conspiracies to each other as they swell with heat. *Tick tick tick*, the grandfather

112

clock insists over the low, humming indignation of the television audience. In the distance, a dog howls its significance into the gathering night. Upstairs, in the room where the girl grew up, not a sound.

The silence terrifies her. Shouldn't she have heard by now? The clock on the television reads 5:53. Her husband will be arriving soon. How will she contain herself if the call comes after this? If the call does not come —?

*Tick. Tick. Tick.*

Her eyes burn into the toy-red telephone on the coffee table and she begs the gods *brahma vishnu mahesh* to bring it to ring, the deities who are perhaps within closer range, *ganesha krishna rama*, but such immediate results were apparently not in her stars. She picks up the receiver and, each finger quick with its own pulse, presses redial.

*Hello and happy new year! Miranda, Dana, and Kayla aren't in right now, but if you leave us your name, number, and the time you called —*

She hangs up.

She had longed to name her Kala, which meant *phases*, but her husband did not like the word much because it also meant *black*. He decided Kayla would be just Americanized enough a name to allow the girl a smooth assimilation into this strange atmosphere, so sharp and bright it bounced off things, and so unlike the slow Bombay haze, heavy and sweet with the smoke of a thousand cow-dung fires, which burned through the hospital walls and into her small new body when first she gasped her way into the world. It was a well-intentioned but resistant breed of assimilation he sought for Kayla: he wanted her to have the finest *salwar kamees* to celebrate her first day at school, then was

113

perplexed even when she came home trembling because of how the blue-jeaned children had laughed and stared with cool blue eyes; he wanted her to attend the best of universities, even if this meant allowing her a life in her very own time zone, so she could eventually land a parallel-quality job until the finest of Indian men, perhaps a surgeon from Delhi, would enter her life and relieve her of these temporarily necessary but ultimately undesirable circumstances. However, in the limbo hours after the class dance in June, he was devastated to find that she'd dabbled as well in the finest of wine coolers, two liters of knee-bending Sun Country, a discovery he made when she wandered in at two in the morning on the arm of a schoolmate of questionable repute, and proceeded to collapse in votive position at the downstairs toilet.

—I am greatly disappointed in you, he managed to proclaim three days later when his power of speech was restored to him.

—Kayla, she told her then, squatting in the pool of tiled moonlight and grasping the shoulders of the girl who was staring, bewildered, at what she was creating in the porcelain bowl. — You have deeply hurt your father and you have hurt me. We did not think you would be like them; we did not think you would think you had to. Tell me why, just tell me, tell me why.

—I want so much, the girl said, and began to sob.

The woman wanted to tell her, That's all right, we are all creatures of desire and must be strong enough to recognize that, that is what I want for you, that is what is too late for me — but she felt she should be angry and was only very, very sad.

—I know, was what she finally said. —I know. But be careful, Kayla, what you dream, because you must follow the footpaths your dreaming discovers.

Kala meant *phases*. She thought it would have been a fine pairing with her own name, Shashi, which meant *moon*. Her name, actually, had been Shashikala; her mother, in a crystalline moment, crouched on the kitchen cement at Powai Lake, coaxing the threads of fish bone from the pomfret, told her a fading tale of the moon's luminous motion. Desire, devotion, and distance, the healing powers of the sea. Shashikala; her almost-husband had not liked the clunkiness of it at the time and the "Kala," without much discussion, had long ago been dropped so that she remained, simply, the moon. A silver ball cast still in its bounce, never changing its angle to the sun. She did not want that stillness for her daughter. She wanted her to run, stretch, fluctuate. To burst out of the hard rind of earth from its molten center, like the high defiance of trees, the insouciant joy of the geyser.

—I know this is right, Kayla told her one night not so long ago when it was very warm in California and the stars loosened themselves from their constellations and fell, burning. —I dreamed this: that in the whole of the world there is no one like him. I miss him even when he sleeps.

—Be careful, Kayla, she said.

—You always told me to follow my heart.

—But be able to find your way back.

—Maybe, the girl said slowly, —there's no coming back now.

—Dear God, Kayla, she said. —Dear *ram, prubhu, Kayla.*

Her palms are etched with the lines that tell this moment: 5:55. The telephone does not ring and her husband will be home any minute, climbing the drive and emerging from this night, black

115

with failed stars. She knows they surely will have strapped the girl down by now, given her a Valium and a vocabulary with which to justify her situation. She knows how the girl will be in the position she was in when she believed it was love that put her there, and that today is the cold metal day she will begin to believe more and more in evolution and power struggles and in nothing in particular.

She wants to dry her hands but does not want to soil the layers of white cotton in her lap. She thinks of the girl's certain pain and squeezes her palms together in the space where her thighs meet; she closes her eyes and remembers the girl, who passes through history, spiraling. At eighteen she is a disembodied voice, long-distance from California, seventeen and the bottled-up longing, the dream of the garden of Asoka and how it matched the ancient texts though she had never been there, nor read them. Sixteen and candles on a high white cake, downward she grows, ten and fairy tales in the bathtub, the hard, curved pages of drying books, nine, eight and tumbling from the monkey bars, five and befriending the stray spotted dog, four and the dream of the stray spotted dog. Three wrapped in a thick forest quilt, staring just beyond the woman's shoulder into the endless night of the corridor. Two and naked and dancing with the hem of the woman's sari in a Brookline apartment, one, zero, everything at once and the crying subsides as she glides in the silver liquid back between the legs of the woman.

The delivery had been agonizingly solitary. The Bombay hospital was understaffed and her husband had had an emergency of his own to attend to. They had not yet known each other well, the man and the woman, and loved each other shyly and without grace. But this she knew even then: that he was a

116

man with fixed ideas and a good heart and thus a conviction that was at worst naïveté that stills itself into obduracy, at best an immutable innocence. She learned this in a dream in which she was swimming inside him, and in the unfolding distance she saw a heart like the valentines faraway children drew for their mothers, and it was his; she entered it and in its center inside the round tin where her mother kept her jars of coriander, cumin, tamarind at Powai Lake she found a heart like a raw fruit but heavy and thudding and it was hers. He knew nearly the same things: that when he had heard her singing on the class picnic with her hair loose and winding down her back like great twists of black seaweed he would love her someday and, indeed, they grew into love, the love of traveling companions who have only each other and who drift for year upon year into each other's dream states, and wake in a mingled warmth. Now they know each other like the colors of their childhood, for these colors are the same.

But then they were like two strangers whom the gods had with their typical mix of wisdom and whimsy tossed together to take a trip to America for life. In her second-floor Brookline flat, many months later, she passed the day in little acts of waiting for him. He worked long hours. His back had never ached before and now it did, each vertebra straining. He came home when the girl, so tiny then, had already eaten and been sleeping for two hours, and he watched her from the bedroom doorway, standing in the darkened corridor so as not to wake her. He stood there for a long time each night and, from the kitchen sink behind, she watched him; his shoulders stooped with exhaustion. Then he took his seat at the fold-out table and crumbled the speckled leaves of *papad* between his callousing

117

fingers and spoke of the day when they would return to India and help it in its healing, all the hungering masses who squatted at roadside stands to have teeth pulled and cataracts slipped free by a needle's point. He would ask her if she believed in him and she would clear the two dishes and two bowls from the table, pull up a chair, and rub Vaseline into his hands. His palms, cracked with drying rivers and the rivers told her the tale of his wanting; in the morning, he left two hours before the little girl woke up. For many years it was like this. Later, in the New England town where they now live, when his daughter would bump into him before school, blow-drying her hair or lighting the eye pencil to a glide with a long thin match, he would look at her, stunned and with a heart that sang a silver song in his hair and pulled his mouth down with regret; the woman saw this and, fingers bumping from bead to bead, asked that his pain be eased, and that the girl miss none of life's motion.

She thinks now of the sea of evergreens outside her window, and the sweep of frosted night between them, and feels a pang for the narrow, defined spaces of the Brookline flat. When they lived there, some afternoons Aruna would come up to visit. Aruna was her first-floor neighbor who had then been abroad from Delhi a savvy two years. The woman would stand at the stove and brush the bangs from the unblinking eyes of the little girl and boil whole milk and crushed cinnamon and clove for masala tea.

—She looks just like a Beatle, Aruna had said the first time she saw the girl.

—What an odd thing to say. Is that idiom? the woman had asked.

—The Beatles, Aruna had said, then laughed her worldly

118

laugh and strummed her stomach with shell-pink fingernails.
—They are coming from London. They are famous. They
make rock 'n' roll and they are veritable sweepers of the nation.
You know. *Yeah, yeah, yeah.*

She had not asked exactly what this intriguing profession
entailed, and the milk had hissed its way through the sieve and
into the cup of her wise and good and only friend.

—Yeah, yeah, yeah, the little girl had said. The woman
had smiled and pulled her into the folds of her sari.

—Well, she had said, smoothing the damp bed of tea
leaves in the sieve. —She *will* be famous.


—He's going to be famous, Mummy. He studies visual arts and
persuasive communication. He knows the streets of the cities
I've dreamed of. He describes them to me and it's all right,
everything, even the angle of the moon falling by Delacroix's
studio. The abandoned castle in Kaiserswerth. The Cotopaxi.
Petra. He reads Nietzsche.

—Who?

—Yes! You see? He brushes the hair out of my eyes. Do
you see? He doesn't laugh at me.


Her face hotter than the baked pavements of Bombay, she
began the immense process of delivering the girl to the world;
hair matted against her cheeks in dewy tendrils, and with the
fervor of the devout and the terrified, she had longed for her
own mother, Kayla's grandmother, who at that moment would
be receiving the news from Parthav the Patel boy, barefoot
and dusted by the Powai streets he had run through, the Patels
who had the only telephone for miles and, in her haste to slip

into her *chappals*, she would catch her foot on the threshold, slip, and fracture her hip, which would lead to a series of not-so-serious illnesses culminating in the semiserious one that would endure and eventually kill her in the same hospital where her daughter, now Kayla's mother, was at that moment lying, dividing, and longing for her.

Only nights before:
— I had to tell you. Anyway, I thought you knew.
— You are so far, Kayla, so far. How would I have known?
— Somehow.
— I had dreams. I did not understand them before.
— Yes, it can be like that, the girl said, and her breathing was uneven, shivered upward. — It's funny the way things turn out, sometimes, isn't it.

In the sandalwood frame next to the clock which reads 5:58 is the picture that she cannot look at. It is a picture of the most beautiful girl in the whole world on her sixteenth birthday, a girl with eyes the soft shade of cinnamon in the cake candle-light, a rush of dark hair tumbling from her head. The woman looked like her once; the remains of the older generation from Powai Lake say she still does. In the photograph, the girl is blowing and laughing at the same time so that her lips are puckered in a whistling grin. She is making a wish.

— I wish I had listened to you, Mummy, she said last night.
— Had I only known what to tell you.
— I can't believe this is happening.

120

—Tell me there has been some kind of mistake, *ram*, tell me, what have I done?

—And I know. I just know. I've seen him. I must have been dreaming, but I wasn't asleep. He has sticks and toys and pebbles and is very small. He is looking for someone to play with.

—Oh, Kayla, she said. —Oh, my baby.

She knows what he looks like, too. She, too, has seen him. In fact, earlier that afternoon as she was carrying the wicker basket of whites into the laundry room she heard a tapping on the sliding glass door and turned and there he was on the back porch by the fallen shovel, his face pressed to the glass as if to a candy shop vitrine. In his hand was a stick of fluted wood. His smallness and pallor were striking against the backdrop of evergreens and his eyes had all the sad, yellowing radiance of late-summer fruits. He was shivering; instinctively, she bent to unlock the door, and when she looked up there was the porch and shovel, trees shouldering snow-heavy sky. There was the laundry basket toppled by her feet. She was dizzy and crouched to collect the fallen linen.

She knows how the girl dreams. She knows how the girl has dreamed of cross streets in other neighborhoods and dining rooms where hanging lamps shed oil around brass Athenas, and has later found herself at these crossings, these suppers with people she never before knew. She knows how the girl will now fill her mind with images of the snow drifts where she used to make angels and birthday cake icing, but how she will cringe and turn from the sight of it anyway, how later the boy will say all the things she wants to hear and it won't be what she wants. The incense ashes its way down the stick, the house grinds out a bleak sonata of cold and hot and cold. The hissing, clinking, tap *tick tick*ing: all are the sounds of the telephone not ringing. These sounds will drive her mad. She begins to breathe in one, two, out one, two. She counts aloud in the empty house, puncturing the fundamental silence. Through the window, the moon rises.

—One. Two. One. Two.

She stops. There is a new sound from somewhere between the howling dog and where she sits. First it is the sound of tires upon gravel and then it is the sound of a dying engine, footsteps stamping snow on a mat, and then a door, sliding.

—Shashi! from just beyond the kitchen.

She leaps to her feet, and an afternoon of folding and refolding is ended. The handkerchiefs come undone, thousands it seems, drifting like leaves too soon from weary trees. The handkerchiefs pile in snowy drifts around her ankles and snow collects upon the thin edge of fence off of which the boy, startled by a sound in a distant house, in a world nearly close, is toppling, his fluted stick whirling in the air, his curls unwinding like a swimmer's in an undertow. On another coast, dreaming upward from her ache, the girl leans far into the night and tries with a last might to fling her arms around the moon, but she is entangled in waves of hair and white sheets and like a great silver ball it is bouncing, bounding just out of reach.

—Shashi, I'm home.

In the house, at six o'clock, the telephone begins to ring.

# JACK AND DEAN

## by Kevin Brooks

I first met Dean in 1975 when we were both fifteen. It was half-way through the summer term when he showed up at school. No one knew who he was or where he came from; he just walked into the classroom one day, alone and unannounced, and sat himself down at a desk.

All the other kids, including me, pretended not to notice him. He was a new kid. You don't talk to new kids, do you? You just carry on doing what you're doing, which in our case wasn't much. It was the first period after the midmorning break, and we were all just hanging around waiting for the art teacher to arrive. The classroom was noisy, but not too noisy. Chaotic, but not too chaotic. Most of us were just sitting around talking, trying to look cool, or standing over by the window watching the girls from the convent school across the road. We all kept looking over at Dean, of course, flicking sly glances in his direction, checking him out, but he didn't seem to care. He just sat there, cool as you like, sucking the end of a pencil and gazing calmly around the classroom, weighing things up.

\*      \*      \*

Even then, before we'd spoken a word to each other, I knew there was something special about him. I didn't know what it was, and I wasn't even sure if I liked it or not, but I knew it was something I couldn't resist.

He was a lean and hard-looking kid. He had a pale and angular face, dirty blond hair, and eyes that burned green. When he smiled it made your skin tingle.

He was smiling now, I realized. Smiling to himself as he fixed his eyes on a kid called Davis who was standing over by the window, mouthing off about something to anyone who'd listen. Davis was the hardest kid in school. He wasn't that big, or even that strong, but he was vicious. A bit mad, too — a bit of a psycho. I remember once, when we were queuing up for lunch, this kid called Ross bumped into Davis by mistake and spilled a can of Coke on him. Ross tried to apologize, but Davis didn't want to know — he just smiled coldly, pulled a knife from his pocket, and stuck it in Ross's thigh.

Just like that.

Didn't even blink.

Just stabbed him and walked away.

Crazy as hell.

Anyway, Dean was watching Davis now. Watching him like a hawk. I wasn't sure if Davis was aware of it, but it was obvious to me that something was about to happen. I could feel the tension in the air. It felt dark and electric, like the uneasy silence before a thunderstorm. Some of the other kids were beginning to notice it, too, and as they stopped talking, others stopped talking, and within a few minutes the whole classroom had gone quiet. Everyone was watching, waiting, their eyes flicking expectantly between the new kid and Davis.

Dean didn't move for a while. He didn't do anything. He just sat there, soaking up the growing attention, still smiling to himself, still staring, still looking calm. His eyes had cooled to a pale green shimmer of ice.

He waited until the silence was almost complete and then — without a word — he got to his feet, strode across the classroom, and punched Davis full in the head — *SMACK!* It was incredible — the power, the shock, the sickening crack. It was like something out of a film. Davis's head jerked back and he fell to the floor like he was dead. And for a heart-stopping moment, I thought he *was* dead. I couldn't see any movement. He wasn't groaning or sighing or holding his head — he was just lying there, flat on his face, as lifeless as a broken doll.

*My God*, I thought, *he's dead. The new kid's* killed *him*. But then — just as I was beginning to imagine the worst — I saw Davis's foot twitch. It wasn't much, just a tiny little movement, but it was good enough for me. It was good enough for Dean, too. Satisfied that Davis was still alive, he yanked him to his feet and proceeded to beat the living shit out of him.

I'd never seen anything like it. Dean's fists were like hammers — *bam bam bam* . . . *smack smack smack* — mashing Davis's face to a pulp. It was *awesome*. Everyone in the class room was too shocked too move. All we could do was stand there, amazed, as Dean kept thundering his fists into Davis's head — *bam bam bam* . . . *smack smack smack* — over and over and over again. And all the time, Dean never said a word. Never cursed. Never shouted. Never made a sound. He never

125

even grunted. He just kept on beating on Davis, pounding away without mercy, until the teacher came in and pulled him off and angrily dragged him away.

I remember a lot of things about that day. I remember looking around at the other kids and seeing the dazed looks on their faces, and I remember the nurse coming in and cradling Davis's bloody head in her arms. But most of all I remember Dean looking over his shoulder and smiling at me as the teacher led him out of the classroom.

He looked as innocent as a child.

The next day, after school, I was walking down to the bus station when I heard someone coming up behind me. At first I thought it was some older kids who'd been bothering me over the last few weeks, and my heart began to pound. I started walking faster, hoping I was wrong, and then a friendly voice called out from behind me.

"Hey, hold on . . . just a minute . . ."

I turned round, and there was Dean, bopping along with his hands in his pockets and a big goofy grin on his face.

"All right?" he said.

"Uh . . . yeah," I replied hesitantly.

The next thing I knew, Dean was walking along beside me, grinning like a mad thing and bombarding me with questions: what's your name? where d'you live? what kind of music d'you like? what d'you read? where d'you go? what d'you do?

It was hard to keep up with him. He walked fast, talked fast . . . he never stopped moving. Bobbing up and down all the time, nodding and swiveling his head like a boxer waiting for the bell, waving his arms all over the place. His eyes didn't keep still for a second — looking up, looking down, flashing from side to side . . .

It was exhausting just being with him.

Confusing, too.

I didn't know what to do. I didn't know what he wanted from me. I didn't know what to say. I considered asking him about Davis, about why he'd beaten him up, and what the headmaster had said about it . . . but somehow it didn't seem the right thing to do.

Either that, or I was just too scared.

And I *was* scared, no doubt about it. It was a scary situation. The only thing I knew about this strange kid from nowhere was that yesterday he'd hammered Davis to a pulp, and now he was walking along beside me, asking me questions, jabbering away like a lunatic.

Yeah, it was *scary* . . .

But it was kind of exciting, too.

Like playing with fire.

"Where're you going?" he said.

"Bus station," I told him.

He nodded. "You wanna come over to my place?"

"What — now?"

He shrugged. "Whenever."

"Yeah . . . I mean, not now —"

"You know the Green Farm Estate?"

"Yeah."

"Twenty-eight Pentecost Road . . . okay?"

"Right. . . ."

He grinned at me, then skipped to one side and put his foot

up on a wall to tie his shoelace. I stopped beside him. He was quiet for a moment, concentrating on his laces, tying them in weird double knots, and as I stood there watching him I couldn't help noticing his sneakers — they were big fat black things with inch-thick soles.

"Cool shoes," I said.

"Yeah, yeah," he replied. "You wanna get some. They're good for bouncing." And with that, he jumped across the pavement, leapt in the air, and slapped his hand against the side of a passing bus — *WHAP!* He pushed himself off the bus, twisted in midair, and landed in a crouch in the gutter, grinning up at the sight of a shocked old lady who was wagging her finger at him through the bus window.

"See?" he said to me, straightening up and tapping the sole of his sneaker.

"Yeah," I said. "That's bouncy, all right."

We carried on walking.
Dean carried on talking.
I carried on listening.

He told me about this girl he'd seen, sunbathing nude in the garden next door to him. He told me she knew he was watching her. He told me he'd been to America — *the States*, he called it. He told me he was moving to London next year — *the Smoke*. He told me he played the guitar, and I told him that I did, too.

"I'm not very good —" I started to say.

"Doesn't matter," he said. "Bring it over when you come

128

round; we'll play some stuff together. What is it — electric or acoustic?"

"Just an acoustic."

"Yeah, me, too. I'm getting an electric soon, though — a Fender. Then we can *really* make some noise. . . ." He mimed a big power chord and yelled out "*Kerrang!*" — waving his arms about and jumping in the air, screaming guitar sounds at the top of his voice.

A passing kid gave him a dirty look.

Dean looked at him and said, "What? You got a problem?"

The kid shook his head and walked on.

When we reached the bus station at the bottom of the hill, Dean touched me on the shoulder and said, "Okay, I gotta go. I'll see you tomorrow — all right?"

"Yeah . . . right."

He grinned at me again, stamped his foot up and down, and then he was gone, bouncing and bobbing his way up a side street, fading away into the distance like the trailing light of a dying star.

And that was the start of it, I suppose — the start of me and Dean. It was a strange experience for me, because I'd never really had a close friend before. I'd had friends, of course — kids I hung around with, kids I grew up with, that kind of thing — but we'd never really meant that much to each other. We were only friends because we had things in common — we were the same age, or we lived near each other, or we went to the same school . . . what you might call friendships of convenience.

129

With Dean, though, it was different.

We still had the usual things in common — we were both fifteen, we both went to the same school — but we had other things in common, too. Different things. Real things. Things that mattered. With us, it wasn't just a case of seeing each other because there wasn't anything better to do; we *wanted* to see each other. And it wasn't always easy, either, because Dean lived miles away from me, right across the other side of town, which meant we had to make an effort to see each other. But the thing is, we *wanted* to make the effort. We *wanted* to be together. Not just at school, but at other times and other places, too. After school, evenings, weekends, the park, the town, the streets, his house . . .

God, Dean's house.

I couldn't believe it the first time I went round there. It was about a week after I'd first met him. I had to get a bus from my place to town, then another bus up to the Green Farm Road, and then a long rambling walk up to the estate. It was one of those developments where all the houses and all the roads look the same, so it's really easy to get lost . . . which I did. More than once, in fact. But I got there eventually — Pentecost Road — and I found Dean's house. When I rang the bell he answered almost immediately, dragging me inside and showing me into the front room. It was a fairly small house, a lot smaller than mine, and the rooms were packed with all sorts of stuff — books, pictures, weird ornaments — which made it seem even smaller.

Anyway, Dean introduced me to his mother, who was sitting on the floor threading some beads on a necklace, and then we both sat down on a dusty old settee that was covered with a patchwork blanket. Dean started talking to me, asking me about my journey or something, but I wasn't really listening to what he was saying. I was staring at the cigarette in his hand. I couldn't believe it. He was smoking a *cigarette* . . . right in front of his mother. As he carried on talking to me, I kept glancing at her, waiting for her to do something, but she didn't say a word. She just sat there, concentrating on her beads, smiling quietly to herself, while her son puffed away.

At one point, she even passed him an ashtray.

Unbelievable.

I learned afterward that she used to be an actress or a singer or something. She wore floppy old hippie clothes and smoked roll-ups in an ebony cigarette holder, and she was always drinking wine. She'd cook up strange, exotic, spicy food that we ate from bowls as we sat on the floor. And she'd swear at Dean, too — and he'd swear back at her, telling her to eff off.

It was all very different to what I was used to.

But I liked it.


Thinking back on it now, there was so much I didn't know about Dean, and so much I never found out. I often wonder why I never asked him more about his life. *What happened to your dad? How does your mom make a living? Where do you come from? Why did you move here?*

The questions just didn't occur to me.

I never even got round to asking him why he beat up Davis. I think I know, though. I think he worked out that Davis was the hardest guy around, and he knew that if he beat him up he'd never get any trouble from anyone else. And he was right. After that first day, no one so much as *looked* at Dean the wrong way.

Anyway, I suppose I never asked him too much about himself because, in a funny kind of way, I knew it didn't matter. Maybe I'm just kidding myself, but I'm sure we both knew that something was going to happen back then.

Dean, I think, always knew that he was going to die.

He lived his life as if nothing mattered. He had no regard for anyone or anything, least of all himself. It was almost as if he was dancing with the absence of his future, playing twisted games with it, making the most of what little he had. He did everything with abandon. Too much, too fast, too loud, too dangerous. I think, deep down, that he was torn with bitterness, but he was determined not to let it get in the way, and I'm sure that at least some of his happiness was genuine.

It was a good time for him to live a short life.

And me? Well, I knew that I was going to be something — a writer, a poet, a rock 'n' roll star — and I knew that Dean was going to take me there. In the same way that he needed me, I needed him. He showed me a different world, a world of thrills and danger and excitement. He was my ticket to the circus, my antihero, my pet monster. And I was his . . .

His what?

I still don't really know what I was to Dean. His last companion, perhaps? His dream of life?

Or maybe I was just his Jack, as he was my Dean.

But all that came later.

That first summer we were just two teenagers, doing the stuff that teenagers do. It was a pretty good time, no matter how it turned out in the end, and me and Dean made the most of it.

Sometimes we'd just sit around in his bedroom for hours, smoking cigarettes and talking about stuff — sex and drugs and girls and guitars — and all the time Dean's sound system would be cranked up good and loud, thrashing out the music we liked: loud stuff, rocky stuff, thrashy stuff. If we found something we really liked, we'd play it over and over again, playing along with our guitars, dreaming our dreams.

"We could do this, you know," Dean would often say. "We could get a band together. Me on vocals, you on guitar —"

"*You* on vocals?"

"Yeah."

"Why not me?"

"You can't sing."

"Neither can you."

"Yeah." He grinned. "But I've got the guts. I can *do* it. And I'm better-looking than you."

I don't know about the looks, but he was right about the guts. Nothing scared him, nothing bothered him. He didn't care what other people thought. He could stand up and do anything he wanted to do.

And he did.

Sometimes it scared the hell out of me.

Dean's violence was always there, always boiling up inside him, just waiting to explode. Once I saw him grab a little kid in the gym and smash his head against the wall bars. When I went up to Dean afterward and asked him what was going on, he stared at me as if I was a total stranger, spat on the floor, then walked out and slammed the door.

He only ever hurt me — physically — twice. Once when

133

we were pretending to fight in his back garden, and he got carried away and punched me hard in the head, and another time when I was sitting in the locker room at school and he just walked in and kicked me viciously in the knee, then turned round and walked out again.

I never found out why he did that.

But physical pain isn't the only way to hurt someone, and Dean was fully aware of that. He knew how to be nasty. He knew how to find your weakness, and how to exploit it, and he had the coldness and the determination to keep on picking away at it, over and over again, and sometimes it was almost impossible to bear . . .

But I did.

I put up with it.

I don't know why.

But I did.

And I think Dean admired me for that.


Most weekends we'd get up early and head off somewhere, looking for something to do. Sometimes we'd take a bus or a train, but most of the time we just walked. We'd cadge some money from somewhere, strap our guitars to our backs, and start walking. It didn't matter where we went — anywhere would do. We'd pick a place — a town or a beach or somewhere — and then we'd just head off in that direction and see what happened.

What happened, usually, was nothing. But that was okay. We were happy enough just wandering around, checking things out, looking at the girls on the beach, drinking cups of coffee . . .

And then, at the end of the day, we'd walk back home with aching legs and blistered feet, tired and happy, our dreams intact.

It was one of those long hot summers that seems to last forever. And sometimes I think that maybe it did.

I remember one day in particular. We were sitting cross-legged by the pond in the park, soaking up the sun after school, and Dean was fixing together some Rizla papers on the back of his biology book, trying to roll a joint. We didn't have anything to put in it, but that didn't seem to matter.

Dean's hair was cut short now, hacked into thick chunky spikes, and his fingernails were flecked with black nail varnish.

I watched him as he stuck another Rizla into the giant paper jigsaw. It was a complete mess. I wasn't sure how it was supposed to look, but it didn't look right to me. Dean angled his head and peered at it for a moment, then he swore quietly, screwed the papers into a ball, and chucked it in the bushes.

"I thought you said you knew how to do it," I said.

He looked at me and shrugged — so what? — then he leaned backward until he toppled over and lay on his back looking up at the sky.

"So," he said, "when d'you wanna go then?"

"Go where?"

He turned his head to the side and spat. "St. Ives — the caravan."

He'd been telling me about this trailer for ages. It belonged to his sister's boyfriend, apparently. The boyfriend was away for the summer, so it was empty and available. The idea was, we'd take the bus to Exeter, where Dean had some friends, stay there for a few days, then go on down to Cornwall where we'd live in this caravan for a week or so, like beach gypsies. We'd go beach-combing, cook up sausages on a campfire, get drunk, and go swimming at night . . . that was the idea, anyway.

"I dunno," I said. "When do *you* want to go?"

"I dunno," replied Dean. "When do *you* wanna go?"

Just then, a gaggle of sixth-form girls walked by on the path beside us. We both watched them for a while, thinking our thoughts, then one of them looked over at us and giggled, and Dean raised his leg in the air and farted loudly. The giggling girl looked away and moved on.

"So," said Dean, turning back to me. "When d'you wanna go?"

A couple of weeks later, on a blazing hot day, we were perched on the back of a bus station bench, waiting for the West Country bus to arrive. The bus station was crowded with people and thick with the smell of suntan lotion and exhaust fumes. Green-and-white buses lurched and rumbled around the concourse, slotting in and out of their diagonal parking bays, and the bus drivers — in their sunglasses and their sweat-stained bus driver shirts — were leaning out from their cabs and yelling to one another in the heat. Behind us was a row of cheap dirty offices with dusty windows and bus-colored doors. Inside the offices, birdlike women were tapping away on key-boards, and a bald bus station manager was leaning against a filing cabinet eating a pork pie.

"What a life," sneered Dean.

"What?"

"Him," he explained, nodding at the bus station manager. "Stuck in a crappy little office all day — I mean, what's the point?"

"Maybe he likes it," I suggested.

Dean was about to reply when a bus swung into the concourse and pulled into the bay in front of us. The sign over the driver's cab said *Penzance*.

We grabbed our bags and jumped off the bench and marched off toward the coach, Dean in front — as always — and me tagging along behind. Dean was dressed in a plain black T-shirt with the sleeves torn off, tight black jeans, and dirty blue basketball boots. I was wearing pretty much the same, except my T-shirt had a picture of a skull on the front and my basketball boots were black. We were both wearing cheap plastic sunglasses.

We got on the bus, showed our tickets to the driver, and shuffled up the aisle to the backseat. As soon as we'd sat down, Dean started messing about with the emergency door handle — tugging it, pulling it, whacking it. Suddenly, the door swung open and a buzzer sounded, and the driver shouted down the aisle — "Oi! You at the back — shut the bloody door and leave it alone or I'll throw you off the bus."

Dean grinned and gave him the finger.

"Shut the door, Dean," I said.

"Why?"

"Because if you don't, we're never going to get anywhere."

He thought about it for a moment, then grabbed the handle and closed the door.

*　　*　　*

137

It took ages to get out of town. The bus kept stopping and starting, crawling along through the busy city streets, but eventually we got going, and then pretty soon we were racing along the motorway, heading for the West Country.

I was happy enough just staring out the window at the passing fields and towns, watching out for glimpses of the sea, but Dean was too hyperactive to sit very long without doing anything, and he couldn't stop talking about his friends in Exeter. "Ron and Don are pretty cool," he told me. "Kinda weird . . . but cool. Ron plays guitar in a punk band. I dunno what Don does. He's all right though — he's Ron's brother. Looks just like him, just as weird. They've got this flat in a big old house full of punks and junkies. There's always something going on there — parties and music and stuff. I saw Ron's group once — dunno what they're called — they were supporting someone pretty big . . . can't remember who. They play really fast and loud. We should do that, Jack . . ." He flicked me on the side of the head to make sure I was listening. "Hey, Jack."

He always called me Jack. I'd told him that first day that my name was John, but he always called me Jack.

"What?" I said.

"We should get that band together. What d'you think?"

"Yeah," I said.

He started to beat a twelve-bar blues rhythm on the back of the seat in front of us, then he started making guitar noises — *dunka dunka dunka dunka* — and then he started singing. His voice was pretty good by now, but the words he was singing weren't all that nice, and some of the other passengers started looking round at us. Dean stopped singing and stared back, bug-eyed and dangerous. They all looked away.

The bus rolled on.

Dean reached down and picked his bag up off the floor. Turning to me with a leering grin, he gave the bag a quick shake. Bottles clinked. He unzipped it and held it open for me to see inside. I saw bottles of cheap wine, a six-pack of beer, and half a dozen packets of caffeine pills. Dean popped a couple of cans and broke out a handful of tablets and we both stooped down behind the seats to guzzle down the caffeine pills with mouthfuls of warm beer. The combination didn't taste too good — kind of harsh and bitter and malty — but we chased it all down with a few slugs of wine, which made things a lot sweeter, and then we got talking.

We talked to each other about everything and nothing. I told Dean about all the things I wanted to do, about all the poems and books and plays I was going to write, and he listened to me and nodded his head up and down and urged me on with hundreds of *yes*es and *right*s and *good*s, and then he told me lots of stories about all the sex he'd had and all the fights he'd been in and all the terrible things he'd done . . . and it didn't matter if any of it was true or not, because we were both living a life of dreams and stories, and that was all we wanted.

After a while I think I must have dozed off. When I woke up — with a bone-dry mouth and sticky eyes — Dean was carving something into the back of the bus seat with his penknife. He was quiet for once . . . quiet and calm. He didn't know that I was watching him, and I could see the striking sadness that showed in his face when his mask was down. He looked tired and young and fearful.

I read the words he'd hacked into the back of the seat. They said — *Jack & Dean 4 Ever*.

When he realized that I was awake, a flicker of embarrassment crossed his face, but it only lasted a moment. The mask came up, the sadness disappeared, and the carefree Dean was soon back in action. He leaned back in his seat, snapped his penknife shut, and said in a very loud voice, "God, I need a piss."

"You can't —" I started to say, but he was already out of his seat and striding down to the front of the bus. He stopped beside the driver and said, "Stop the bus, mister — I need a piss."

The driver looked at him like he was a dog turd. "You'll have to wait like everybody else, son."

"No, you don't understand," Dean said coolly, "I *need* a piss. If you don't stop the coach, I'll do it on the floor."

The driver started arguing, but he could tell by the look on Dean's face that he meant what he said, so he pulled the bus into a lay-by and sat fuming in the heat as Dean sauntered off and relieved himself on the grass verge, looking back over his shoulder toward the rest of us with a big mad grin on his face.

When we got going again, Dean opened up another two beers and passed one to me, and then he started to tell me another story, this one about a Frenchwoman he'd met in America who'd filed her teeth into fangs because she wanted to look like a vampire. . . .

We pulled into Exeter sometime in the late afternoon. The sun was still blazing high in the sky, the air was baked, and I was burned out and exhausted. My head was throbbing, my throat was dry, and my chest was as tight as a drum. Dean, though, seemed fine. He jumped off the bus, bouncy as ever, and went to look for his friends, leaving me sitting on another bus station bench, drinking a can of warm Coke.

The bus station looked exactly the same as the one we'd left that morning. Same old people, same old offices, same old bus drivers. The buses were a different color, though, and the people spoke with a funny accent — a thick lazy burr with peculiar inflections and unexpected emphases. Everything they said sounded like a question.

I was beginning to feel out of place now. Out of sorts. Out of something. I didn't know what it was, but I just didn't feel right anymore. I didn't know what I was doing there.

After a while, Dean returned and said that Ron and Don hadn't arrived yet.

"They're probably stoned," he said, smiling at the thought. "Got stoned and forgot all about us."

"Great," I said miserably. "So what are we going to do now?"

"Don't worry about it . . . they'll get here eventually." He looked at me, pulling a face, trying to cheer me up, but I didn't want to be cheered up. All I wanted to do was get out of the damn bus station and go somewhere nice and quiet. "Come on," Dean grinned, playfully putting his arm round my shoulder. "Enjoy yourself — live for the moment."

"Yeah, right," I said. "That's what you're doing, is it?"

He sat back, smiling. "It is at the moment, yeah."

I looked around, taking in the moment — bored faces, litter, broken chocolate machines. I let out a sigh.

Dean said, "You know what your trouble is? You worry too

141

much. You wanna try taking it easy . . . chill out, man . . . lighten up. Worrying about things is a waste of time —"

"Dean," I said. "Shut up."

We decided to wait in the bus station café. It was a big old place, below ground level, at the far end of the bus station. Clouds of cigarette smoke dimmed the light, and the air was stale and lifeless. Rows of stained tables were littered with dirty plates and dirty cups and dirty screwed-up napkins. The floor was sticky and the ceiling was yellow.

We bought coffees and sat by a window looking out onto a drab concrete square. The square was dotted with stunted saplings in rubbish-filled wire bins. On the table in front of us was a squat glass sugar jar, a red plastic ketchup holder in the shape of a tomato, and a big tin ashtray overflowing with cigarette ends. Dean picked up the ashtray and emptied it on the floor.

"Shithole," he muttered, lighting a cigarette.

A waitress looked over at us, glowering at the mess on the floor. Dean stared back at her. She held his gaze for a moment, then looked away.

"Why do you always have to do that?" I asked him.

"What?"

"Annoy people."

He shrugged. "It's fun."

"Not for them, it's not."

"Who cares?" He looked at me, looked over at the waitress, then sniffed hard and spat on the floor.

I nearly got up and left then. I wasn't angry or disgusted or anything, I was just fed up with it all. I'd had enough. Enough of Dean, enough of traveling, enough of drinking and smoking and the constant conflict and the stifling heat . . .

And there was still another week to go.

*Why don't you just get up and say good-bye?* I asked myself. *Just get on a coach and go home . . .*

"Look —" I started to say, but then Dean spotted Ron and Don slouching along outside the café. He stood up and banged his hand against the window and called out to them.

"Don! Ron! Hey!"

They stopped and squinted through the café window, nodded at Dean, then waved us outside, pointing to a dirty white Transit van parked on double-yellow lines across the road.

As we rose to leave, Dean said to me, "What were you saying?"

"When?"

"Just now — you were about to say something."

I looked at him. His eyes were sparkling with excitement.

"Nothing," I told him, shaking my head. "It was nothing. Come on, let's get out of here."


Ron and Don's flat consisted of one big room with a small kitchen on the landing and a shared toilet downstairs. It smelled of stale food and grease and dirty clothes. The floor was hidden beneath a carpet of old newspapers, records, magazines, crusty plates, and overflowing ashtrays. There was a tired and soiled settee, two gray armchairs, and a huge sound system balanced on breezeblocks up against the wall. A bald budgerigar sat morosely in a small birdcage in the corner of the room.

We'd been there for a couple of hours now, and all we'd

done was sit around smoking joints and drinking wine and listening to music. There were five of us — me and Dean, Ron and Don, and a guy called Chief. He'd been driving the van. They called him Chief, Dean told me, because he liked to watch television wearing a Red Indian headdress. He was big, well over six feet tall, with large pale eyes, a shapeless grin, and a medieval haircut. He reminded me of a cartoon character. It was hard to tell if he was friendly or not, because all he did was sit bolt upright in one of the armchairs, sucking red wine from a big tin mug and occasionally chortling — *hur hur hur*.

Ron and Don didn't do much, either. They'd hardly said a word in the van, and now they were just sitting there, slumped side by side on the settee, smoking and drinking, staring at nothing, like a pair of ventriloquist's dummies. They were both tall and dark and, as Dean had promised, they both looked weird. Ron had close-cropped hair, a wide mouth with heavy lips, a flat nose, and small dangerous eyes. His brother looked exactly the same, only slightly thinner. They both wore scabby leather jackets bedecked with pins and chains and badges and scraps of things. Ron's jacket had a child's dummy hanging from a pocket zipper.

Dean, of course, was all over the place, one minute bouncing up and down on his hands and knees, grabbing at cigarettes and bottles, the next minute dancing round the room poking at things on shelves, flipping through records, gawking out of the window.

Me? I just sat on the floor in a daze.

I wasn't used to this kind of thing. I'd never really drunk much before, and I'd never smoked joints at all. My head

was swimming. Cannabis, caffeine, beer, wine, coffee, cigarettes, fear . . .

I was drowning.

I could hear Dean's voice calling out to me from somewhere across the room — "Hey, Jack . . . Jack!" — but he was
too far away, his voice too muffled, too strange. "Look at him,
Ron," I heard Dean say. "Look at his eyes." And his laughing
voice seemed to echo around the room — *his eyes, his eyes, his
eyes* . . .

Everything felt really strange.

Underwater.

Mushy.

Indistinct.

I tried concentrating on the music to clear my mind, but
that only made things worse. It was the most painful music I'd
ever heard — a horrible jarring cacophony that sounded like
eight different groups all playing at once. It hurt my head and
made me feel sick. But the trouble was, once I'd started to listen, I couldn't seem to stop. It was taking me over, getting
louder and louder all the time, swirling and whirling around
the room like a big black cloud, fogging up my head, stinging
my eyes, choking the breath from my lungs, turning my stomach upside down . . .

"Excuse me," I tried to say, attempting to stand up.

But I couldn't stand up.

And I couldn't say "excuse me," either.

All I could say was, "Nunnnhhh . . ."

Then I lowered my head to the floor and threw up.

*     *     *

145

I didn't know what time it was when we left the flat, but I guessed it was quite late because the night was dark and the summer air was turning cold. We all piled into the van — me and Dean in the back, Ron and Don up front, big Chief at the wheel — and then we were off, racing out of town and along the dark country lanes, heading for some pub where a local group was supposed to be playing.

Chief was driving like a crazy man — overtaking on corners, swinging out onto the wrong side of the road, rattling along at breakneck speed — and I genuinely believed I was going to die. *This is it*, I thought with a sinking heart. *This is where it all ends — in the back of a crappy Transit van, drunk and sick and tired and petrified . . .*

*God*, I thought, *I don't even know where I* am.

I turned my head to the side of the van, closed my eyes, and waited for the crash.

It never came, of course.

It was never meant to.

But even now, I still have a mortal fear of driving on dark country roads, and the presence of death that touched me that night is never too far away.

The van raced on like a roller coaster through the dead black night. Dean was still drinking, sloshing down cider from a plastic gallon jug, giggling like an idiot as he leaned drunkenly over the front seat and tried to grab the steering wheel. Ron and Don were still dim and motionless, sitting in the front seat with sick wet eyes. And Chief was still chortling — *hur hur hur*.

146

I pressed my dizzy head into my hands.

Behind my closed eyes, frightening images played through my mind — ghostly trees, looming hedgerows, deserted fields. I could smell petrol and oil, the heat of the engine, and other smells, too — bad smells. Human smells.

I felt so sick . . .

And empty.

I wanted to go home.

The pub was a grim and dirty building set in the middle of nowhere. It had blackened brick walls and dirty windows and a sagging roof of broken slate tiles. There was a small car park of pitted concrete at the front and a patch of bare grass at the back. As we pulled into the car park, I looked around with growing unease. There were a couple of beat-up old vans, a handful of rusted cars held together with body filler, and a dirty-looking VW camper van with paintings of naked women on the side. Leaned up against the wall was a string of dark motorcycles with ape-hanger handlebars and yards of chrome tubing that shone dully in the cold moonlight.

It was a bikers' pub.

As we got out of the van and headed for the door, a shudder ran down my spine.

*This is the most stupid thing in the world*, I thought. *Look at us . . . we're strangers, we're weirdos, we're all out of our heads. This is madness. Bikers hate strangers . . . they hate weirdos . . .*

*And Dean . . . ?*

*A pub full of bikers and Dean?*

*It's suicide.*

But it was too late to stop now, and as Dean pushed open the stiff wooden door and entered the bar, I took a deep breath and followed him inside.

It was a smoky little room, dimly lit, with a wooden bar at one end and a small raised stage at the other. It looked as if we'd missed the group. Apart from a sad-looking drum kit and a lonely microphone stand, the stage was empty.

The bar was crowded and noisy, but as the door creaked shut and the five of us moved inside, everything went quiet. The talking died down, the jukebox stopped, and a roomful of hooded eyes turned in our direction. It was like something out of a Western . . . only worse, because it was real.

Most of the bikers were hunched around a table in a corner, but there were others standing by the jukebox, some at the bar, and one or two just hanging around, leaning against the walls . . . they were all over the place. One of them, sitting with his back to the wall, was a huge haystack of a man, ugly and dirty and covered in tattoos and tattoo scabs. He looked serene and evil. The rest of them were a weaselly-looking bunch, but no less nasty, with lank and oily hair, dead eyes, and sickeningly pale faces. They were all dressed in stained and ripped jeans, dirty black boots, and torn sleeveless denims over studded black leathers. And they were all staring at us.

It was real, all right.

The staring faces, the eyes full of violence and hate, the nightmare vision of black leather, denim, boots, and tattoos . . .

All too real.

*Don't look at them*, I told myself.

*Don't say anything.*

148

*Just keep your head down and hope for a miracle.*

Dean, of course, had other ideas.

"What d'you want?" he asked me.

"Uh?" I muttered, cautiously raising my head.

"What d'you wanna drink?"

"Maybe we should go somewhere else," I suggested quietly.

He looked over at the bikers and ran his fingers through his spiky hair. "You worried about them?"

"No . . . I just thought —"

"They're all right," he said too loudly. "Just a bunch of morons. You don't wanna worry about them."

The bikers kept staring, and my heart kept thumping — harder and harder and harder. It was already pumped up with caffeine and nicotine and cheap wine and beer, and I wasn't too sure it could take any more. I felt sick and scared, and I wanted to be somewhere else, *any*where else . . . but I knew that Dean was in his element — flirting with danger, seeing how far he could push things — and I knew he wouldn't back down. He'd keep on going, like he always did, only this time I had a feeling he was going too far. Staring at the bikers, grinning at them, daring them to make a move.

I just looked at him, unable to speak, silently pleading with him — *just leave it, Dean . . . please . . . just this once . . . please.* But he didn't, of course. He just grinned at me for a moment, enjoying my fear, then he bounced up to the bar, brash as you like, and ordered five pints of lager. While the barman was getting the drinks, Dean turned round, leaned against the bar, and stared across at the bikers again.

I remember thinking how small he looked . . . so small and

pale and delicate . . . like a slip of light surrounded by darkness. But then something seemed to change in him, and suddenly he was the Dean I'd seen on that first day at school — his eyes were as cold as ice, and when he smiled it made your skin tingle.

He was smiling now, I realized. Smiling to himself as he fixed his eyes on the enormous biker and mockingly raised his glass to him.

*Here we go*, I thought. *Here it comes . . . any second now . . .*

But to my surprise, nothing happened.

The big biker just looked at Dean for a moment, grumbled something under his breath, then went back to his drinking. One of the others put some money in the jukebox, rock 'n' roll music came on, people started talking again, and the tension seemed to die down.

I looked over at the bar and saw Dean grinning at me. The look on his face said *See? There's nothing to worry about . . . nothing at all.*


We all went over and got our drinks and took them to a table by the door. As we sat down, I suddenly realized I needed a pee. In fact, I realized that I'd never needed a pee as badly as I did then — I was absolutely *bursting*. But there was no way I was going to the toilet in there . . .

No *way* — I'd rather die.

"You all right?" Dean asked me.

He knew I wasn't.

"I think we ought to go," I said, looking around at the others. It was hard to tell what they were thinking. Chief, I was beginning to realize, had little concept of his surrounding

150

environment — he'd happily sit and guzzle himself stupid just about anywhere. Ron and Don, though, despite their blank faces, were starting to show signs of apprehension.

"What do you think?" I said to them. "Do you think we should go?"

They looked at each other, but didn't answer.

Dean lit a cigarette and grinned at me. "You're pathetic, Jack," he said spitefully, blowing smoke across the table. "You're worse than a f —"

He stopped in midsentence as two of the bikers shuffled past on their way to the restroom, staring down at us with psychotic eyes. One of them was the big one, the one who looked like a haystack.

"All right, boys?" Dean chirped.

They slouched past and disappeared through a dirty white door in the wall.

I can't remember exactly what happened then. I recall a sick feeling in my stomach as Dean stood up and followed the two bikers into the restroom, and I seem to remember an unholy silence as he disappeared through the door, leaving the rest of us just sitting there, not knowing what to do. We knew what was coming, but I don't think we really believed it — until we heard it happening.

The sound of the violence was eerily calm — a distant scuffle, muffled thumps, a faint cry . . . and that was it. The cold and undramatic sound of someone being hurt. It was all over in about fifteen seconds. As I was getting to my feet, the bikers came out of the restroom and went back to their table. They were breathing heavily, and one of them had a thin trickle of blood running from the corner of his eye, but apart from that, you wouldn't have known what they'd just done.

I found Dean on the floor beneath the urinals, slumped against the porcelain wall with his hand clasped tightly to his stomach. He'd been stabbed. I couldn't see much blood, but there was a gash in his T-shirt, and I could see the puncture wound in his skin. His face was drained and white, and his eyes were glazed. He looked like a corpse.

"Jack," he said weakly, trying to smile.

"Shut up," I said angrily, kneeling down beside him.

I didn't know what to do. I didn't feel scared anymore, I just felt sick — sick of Dean, sick of myself, sick of everything. It wasn't supposed to be like this . . . it was supposed to be fun.

It was supposed to be us . . .

Just me and Dean.

And now it was all going wrong.

I started to lift Dean's T-shirt. I didn't have a clue what I was doing, and I didn't know what I could do to help him, but I had to do something. There was a lot of blood now. The stab wound was pulsing, oozing red. His T-shirt was soaked. His jeans were bloody. He was breathing strangely. The blood was coming out fast . . . too fast . . . and I didn't know what to do.

Then the door opened and the bar owner came in. He was a squat little man with a shaved head and heavily muscled arms.

"Get him in the ambulance when it gets here," he grunted. "Then the rest of you — piss off. Nobody saw nothing and nobody knows nothing — all right?"

Before I could answer, he'd turned around and walked out. Dean spat some blood onto the floor and coughed.

"It hurts, Jack," he whispered. "It hurts."

He didn't die — not then. The wound was quite deep, and he'd lost a lot of blood, but after the doctors had stitched him up and kept him in hospital for a couple of weeks, he was soon back on his feet again. And, to most people, he was the same old Dean. Brash, bouncy, annoying, irresistible . . .

But he *wasn't* the same.

He was never the same again.

I knew it, and he knew it.

What I didn't know, though — and what I still don't know today — is why. I don't know why he changed. I don't know what happened to him. I don't *know* if the stabbing had anything to do with his death. I'm pretty sure that it did, but the truth is — the shameful truth is — I just don't know. Did something happen when he was in hospital? An infection? A surgical problem? A complication? Was the injury worse than everyone thought?

I don't know.

And I don't have the courage to find out.

*Does it matter?* I often ask myself. *Does it matter that I don't know?* My head tells me it doesn't. Why should it? What difference does it make? Whatever I know or don't know, he's still dead. And I know that, logically, I'm right, it *doesn't* make any difference at all. But that doesn't stop me hurting whenever I think about it, because I know in my heart that I'm wrong.

\*　　　\*　　　\*

After Dean came out of hospital, we stayed friends of a sort for a while. We even got that group together — Dean singing, of course, and me on guitar. It lasted almost a year, and it was good for a while . . . in fact, it was better than good. It was a dream come true. We were finally doing what we'd always wanted to do . . .

But it turned out wrong in the end.

There was too much . . . I don't know . . . too much other stuff — too much badness, too much aggression, too much too much. I just couldn't cope with it. Dean reveled in it, soaking it all up with a snarl and a curse and a willingness to laugh and spit in other people's faces. He loved it. It was everything he'd ever wanted.

He was going to be a star.

And he almost got there.

We were on the verge of signing a record deal, we had a string of national tour dates lined up, everything was ready . . . and then I told Dean that I didn't want to do it anymore. I wanted to leave the group.

And I did.

The deal was called off, the tour was cancelled . . .

And that was it.

The thing between us was finally destroyed.

Dean said some terrible things to me then, things I've never forgotten. He hurt me more than he'd ever hurt me before. And maybe I deserved it. I'd shattered his dream — our dream. I'd let him down. I'd chickened out at the very last moment, scared of something I didn't understand . . .

I don't know.

Maybe I shouldn't have left? Maybe I should have struggled on, doing something I'd come to hate . . .

Maybe I should have put up with it?

But I didn't.

After that, we just drifted apart.

It was about a year after I last saw him that I heard Dean had died. I was living in a different town by then, and someone sent me a letter — *Remember Dean? The guy who used to sing in your band . . . he died last week . . .*

I cried for a while, sitting alone, remembering things, but it didn't really hit me too hard. I didn't go to his funeral or send flowers or anything. I never got in touch with his mother, either. I don't know why not. I felt bad about it afterward, and I still feel bad about it now, but at the time I just thought — *well, it's over, that's all.*

It was just the two of us.

Just me and Dean.

And now it's over.

But it's not, of course — is it, Dean?

It's never over.

Not while I'm still here.

Because I can see you, right now. I can see you looking down on me. Watching me. Forever young. Your eyes burning green like the heart of a flame. I can *see* you, Dean, smiling to yourself as I write these words . . .

I can still feel my skin tingling.

# PICKING

### by Samantha Schutz

i.

I pick.
I am a picker.
I come home at night
and even though I try not to,
I take off my socks
and pick at my feet.
I peel the nails.
I tear the cuticles.
And even though it hurts
and it sometimes bleeds,
it is relaxing.
When I'm doing it,
time stops. I
want to stop,
but I can't.
Or maybe I don't want to
enough.

I don't just pick at home,
where no one can see.
I do it all day long.
I bite my fingernails
and pick at the cuticles.
I pick at my face —
pimples,
dry skin.

My back is covered with brown spots
where I kept picking
and picking. It's amazing
that anything manages to heal.
Maybe my skin works extrahard
while I'm sleeping —
when I can't get at it.

And it's not only my feet
and my hands
and my face
and my back.
It's my legs.
I search for little ingrown hairs
and scabs
to pick and pull.

I hate that I do it,
but I can't stop.
Or maybe I don't want to
enough.

And then there's the head scratching
and cheek biting.
Not nearly as destructive as the rest,
but still, I can't stop.
Or maybe I don't want to
enough.

I walk around
with things constantly hurting,
things bleeding —
things trying to heal,
despite myself.


ii.


According to the Internet, I
am a self-mutilator.
Calling myself that
is so much more serious-sounding
than calling myself a picker —
so much more dangerous.
I look at the Self-Mutilators Anonymous site
and all the things I do
are listed.

The site says that self-mutilators
*deliberately cause injury to their bodies*
*without the intention of ending their lives.*
Also, *the only requirement for membership*

*is the desire to stop self-mutilating.*
I read on.
There are things listed
that I do not do,
like cutting or burning myself,
tearing out body hair,
swallowing objects,
banging my head against walls,
breaking bones or teeth,
compulsive body tattooing or body piercing,
and excessive cosmetic surgeries.

It makes me feel better
to know that there are people
who do worse things to themselves.
But still,
I know my picking is a problem.
I know
because I've tried to stop
and couldn't.
I've covered my bathroom mirror,
washed my face with the lights off,
worn gloves in the house,
painted my nails with nasty-tasting polish,
sat on my hands,
and thrown out several pairs of cuticle scissors.
None of it has helped.

There is an SMA meeting near my house
and even though I know I have friends who would go with me —

support me —
I think it is important to go alone.


iii.


I am nervous on the way to the meeting.
What will the people be like?
What will they look like?
Will they be men or women,
young or old?
Will they have marks on their faces
like me?
Will their fingers and toes hurt too?
Will they be cutters?
Will I see their scars
or will they be hidden?

The meeting is in a church
and when I walk in,
I feel like people can tell I am Jewish —
that I am not here for God,
that I am here for
a meeting.

As I look for the meeting, a sign,
something, I find the sanctuary.
There is singing,
the kind that echoes
off the cold stone walls.

160

I'd rather go in there —
where it's peaceful
and quietly loud,
but that's not why I am here.
I am here for a meeting.

I am going to have to ask for help.
I am going to have to say,
out loud, why I am here.
I go into the office
and very quietly ask the man behind the desk,
"Where is the meeting?"

In the second it takes for him to respond,
I imagine I am in a drugstore,
at the register, and the cashier's voice
is booming over the loudspeaker,
"Price check on yeast infection cream, register four.
Price check on yeast infection cream,"
and everyone in the store is staring at me.

The man behind the desk casually asks,
"The SMA meeting?"
I think I am going to die,
but at least he didn't say
Self-Mutilators Anonymous —
that would have been worse.

There is another woman behind me.
She is going to the meeting too.

161

She looks normal.
I wonder what she does to herself.
She says she will show me the way
to the meeting room.
We head to the basement
and everything is brown —
the walls, the floor, the doors.
As we go down the stairs, I ask her
how many people come to the meeting.
She says four.
I am going to die.
I thought there would be enough people
that I could just sit in the back,
unnoticed.

Four people.
Four people.
Four people.
Four people.

We get to the room
and she rearranges a few chairs
around a card table.
She asks if this is my first meeting.
I say yes.
I am going to cry.
She tells me about herself,
about how the group works.
I am going to cry.

Then she asks me about myself.
I am crying.

I didn't think I was going to have to talk,
and now I am talking
and crying,
and there are no tissues,
and I only have a quarter of a bottle of water —
not nearly enough,
and this room is hot,
really hot,
and a nearby shelf is piled
with things that do not belong with things —
a box of chess pieces
a plastic cake cover.

When our conversation lulls,
I go to the bathroom for tissues.
When I get back there are two other people —
a woman in her thirties
and a man, maybe fifty.
I didn't expect there to be men.
They both look normal —
people I would never notice.
I look for their scars
and see nothing.
I feel badly for looking
and stare down at the floor.

They ask is this is my first meeting,
and when I say yes
they tell me they are happy I am here.
They welcome me
as I hold a wad of toilet paper
in my hands.

When it is exactly four o'clock,
the woman in her thirties
announces that she will be chairing the meeting.
She is in charge,
but only in the sense that she gets us started.
She reads the opening statement from a piece of paper.
It is a paragraph about who the group is.
Then she says that we will take turns
reading the Twelve Steps
and the Tools of Recovery.
Apparently this is like an AA meeting,
except everything has been modified
to apply to self-mutilators.

The chair reads steps one through three
and then hands the paper to me.
She holds her finger where I should begin.
That was nice.
But how am I supposed to read
when I am crying,
holding soggy toilet paper in my hands?
I read steps four through six:

*4. Made a searching and fearless moral inventory of ourselves.*
*5. Admitted to God, to ourselves, and to another human being*
*the exact nature of our wrongdoings.*
*6. Were entirely ready to have God remove*
*all these defects of character.*

I do not see what these steps have to do with me
or my picking.
I pass the paper to the next person,
pointing at where she should begin.
When we've read all twelve steps,
we take turns reading the Tools of Recovery.
I like these, especially:
*Find a creative use for your time.*
*Exercise regularly to relieve stress.*
*Draw or write down your feelings —*
*don't take them out on yourself.*

Next the chair says
that the woman I met in the office
will be qualifying.
The woman qualifying says her first name
and that she is a gratefully recovering self-mutilator.
The others say hello to her in unison.
I catch on and say hello a second too late.
She speaks about herself,
her addiction to self-mutilation,
her recovery, her occasional abstinence
from picking.

I am crying again,
using the same toilet paper to blot my eyes
and blow my nose.
I am distracted as the woman speaks.
Am I like these people?
Should I volunteer to speak?
If I do, what will I say?

When the woman is done qualifying,
the chair asks if anyone else wants to share.
The man raises his hand
and introduces himself.
He says his first name
and that he is a gratefully recovering self-mutilator.
This time I say hello
at the same time as the others.
He says he has been abstinent
for ten years. I
cannot go ten minutes.
When he finishes speaking,
the woman chairing volunteers to share.

These people don't only talk about picking.
They talk about their jobs,
their families, anything.
Since there are so few of us,
people speak for as long as they want.
They ramble.

A woman comes in late,
and when the chair finishes sharing,
the late woman volunteers to speak.
She rambles too,
but it's different.
She talks about picking
and how she is obsessed
with taking care of her skin.
At first it's interesting,
but her share is endless.
She is whining.
I feel terrible
for thinking that.

When she is done, they all look at me
without trying to look at me.
I am the only one who hasn't shared.
I nod and introduce myself.
After they say, "Hi, Samantha,"
I begin to speak.
"I've been picking since I was a teenager.
I used to pluck my eyebrows
until there were only a few hairs
that neatly lined up into an arch."
I laugh.
No one else laughs.
Usually I make people laugh.
Apparently this is not funny.

"It's just been going on a while
and I hate it.
I hate that I do it.
I hate that my hands constantly hurt."
I look at my hands.
The cuticles are raw.
Shit. I'm crying again.
I stop talking.
I say "thank you"
and they say "thank you" back.

We end the meeting by reading affirmations.
I like these.
These make sense to me —
*I let my body heal.*
*I applaud my willingness.*
*I accept myself exactly how and who I am today.*
*My humor is a sign of my recovery.*

When the meeting is over,
I am exhausted.
I take a taxi even though I am broke
and not that far from home.
How am I going to go home and
not pick?
But how can I possibly go to an SMA meeting
and then come home
and pick?

At home,
I start picking.
Then stop
and remind myself not to —
that it hurts,
that I don't really want to.
It works for a moment
and then my hands are at my face,
my back, my scalp.
It seems impossible
not to.

# SMOKING LESSONS

## by Patricia McCormick

You Couldn't Help But Notice Elizabeth LaRue. She was the one wearing black patent-leather shoes and a boy-band fan club jacket on the first day of school. And even though I was wearing the expression I'd practiced in the mirror all summer before coming to the Lane School — my too-cool-to-be-bothered look — she noticed me, too.

She made a beeline for me in homeroom and started asking questions like one of those guys on *60 Minutes*.

"Are you new?" she said. "Me, too!"

I didn't have time to figure out how she knew I was new if she was, too; I scarcely had time to nod between questions.

"Do you take Spanish?" she said. "Me, too!"

"Are you in Math A or B?" she said. "I bet you're in A. Maybe we can be homework buddies."

"Do you like Justin Timberlake?" Without warning, she burst into the chorus of "Cry Me a River."

I pretended that I'd developed a sudden, intense interest in picking off the nail polish I'd put on the night before. In the meantime, I peeked out from under my bangs to see if anyone was looking.

A knot of blond girls with their uniform skirts rolled up to the same identical height — 2.5 rows of plaid — were giggling and pointing at Elizabeth. I knew what they were saying about her. That she was a dork, that she was a loser, that she was a freak.

I knew because at my old school I was an Elizabeth LaRue. And I wasn't about to let that happen again. Especially not at the Lane School, this private all-girls school that my parents couldn't really afford but which they finally said I could go to after I begged them for a fresh start.

"You wanna walk to Spanish together?" she said.

I shrugged.

"You wanna hang out at lunch?"

Elizabeth LaRue didn't look like other girls at the Lane School. She was pudgy and her bangs were cut straight across high on her forehead. Instead of looking cool or ironic or bored, she had a big, exaggerated smile that looked like it was painted on. She reminded me of a Lego woman. She wasn't the kind of person you sit with on the first day if you're trying to make a fresh start.

"I don't think so," I said.

"That's okay," she said, brightly. "I'm sitting with Tabby, anyhow. Maybe tomorrow."

Tabby, it turned out, was Tabby Lane. She was this superskinny girl with perfectly straight white-blond hair and icy blue eyes. When she wasn't sitting across the lunch table from Elizabeth, Tabby Lane was at the center of the knot of blonde girls with the identically short skirts. She was also one of *the* Lanes, the family that had started the Lane School. I couldn't understand why someone like Tabby Lane ate lunch with someone like Elizabeth, but I decided I needed to be friends with Tabby.

So after a week of trying (usually without success) to avoid Elizabeth in homeroom and Spanish and Math A and a week of eating by myself or skipping lunch and hiding out in a stall in the bathroom so I didn't have to eat by myself, I put my lunch tray down next to Elizabeth's.

"Oooh, goody," she said. "You decided to sit with us after all." She nudged Tabby, who was silently pushing her green beans around on her plate. "Tab, this is Margaret. She's new."

"Meg," I explained to Tabby. "They have me listed as Margaret, but I hate that name."

Tabby Lane peered out from behind a curtain of white-blond bangs that had fallen in a perfectly random, perfectly perfect way across her face. "Whatever."

"Tabby's my cousin," Elizabeth said. She beamed.

Tabby blew out a little puff of air with her lower lip; the hair that had fallen across her face floated in the air for a second, then settled back in place.

"C'mon," Elizabeth said to Tabby. "Eat a little bit more."

Tabby didn't even glance up.

"At least eat some of your salad. Or a carrot stick."

Tabby shot her a look. And I understood then why someone like Tabby Lane ate lunch with Elizabeth. Tabby had some kind of eating disorder. Elizabeth was there to make sure she ate.

As if she could read my mind, Tabby confirmed my theory. "Our parents make us eat together," she said flatly.

Elizabeth turned red. Then she looked down at her lap and tugged on a loose thread on the sleeve of her jacket.

172

Tabby sighed. "How much longer do we have, anyway?" she said, pulling back the sleeve of her uniform blouse. A delicate silver watch, something that looked more like a piece of jewelry than a watch, dangled from her pale, tiny wrist.

"I like your watch," I said.

"This?" She regarded the watch absentmindedly. "It's no big deal. It was, you know, in the family."

I didn't know, but I acted like I did.

She checked the time. "We still have ten minutes," she said. "Let's go have a smoke."

Smoking was forbidden at the Lane School. The penalty, according to the little plaid student handbook, was suspension.

Elizabeth's Lego smile disappeared. "Tab, you know we're not allowed."

Tabby blew on her bangs again. Then she looked at me. "You coming?"

I nodded. I'd never smoked before, but I wasn't going to let a little plaid rule book stand in the way of getting to be friends with Tabby Lane.

I got up and trailed after her, trying to copy the way she scuffed her clogs carelessly across the cafeteria floor. Elizabeth jumped up, too, and followed us, the heels of her patent-leather shoes tapping out what sounded to me like Morse code for SOS.

We followed Tabby out of the cafeteria, down a flight of steps, then down a dark hall next to the music room, until we were in a skinny passageway between the music room and the chapel. At the far end was a nook where choir robes were hanging on a row of pegs.

Tabby peered around the corner. Then she pulled a pack of Marlboros out of her purse. I slipped a cigarette out of the pack just the way she did, then held it between my fingers the way she did.

Elizabeth looked miserable, but she took a cigarette, too, then immediately dropped it on the floor. When she straightened up, her face was red. Her hand was shaking as she put the cigarette in her mouth.

Tabby fished around in her purse and brought out a red plastic lighter. She flicked it expertly and a yellow-blue flame shot up. Then she held the lighter out toward me. I understood, somehow, that this was part of the deal. I had to take the first drag. So I did.

The smoke tickled my throat — it was surprisingly hot — but I held back the urge to cough. I exhaled the way people do on TV.

It was Elizabeth's turn next. She puckered her lips and pulled her cheeks in so that she looked like a fish. Then she sucked on the cigarette. Instantly, her eyes bugged out and she started coughing and choking. Tears ran down her cheeks as she gasped for air.

Tabby looked vaguely amused. Then she lit her own cigarette, drew in a long, deep breath, held it, then exhaled a perfect white stream of smoke.

I made a mental note of how she did this.

Elizabeth dropped her cigarette on the floor and stubbed it out under her shoe. "Sorry, Tab." She shrugged. "I just can't."

Tabby took another drag on her cigarette. I took another drag. Tabby exhaled. I exhaled.

Elizabeth waved her hand in front of her face, trying to fan the smoke away. Then she looked at her watch. "Hurry up," she said. "Big Beef could walk right through here any minute."

Tabby didn't blink.

I didn't know who Big Beef was, but I also didn't blink.

Elizabeth turned to me to explain. "Big Beef is Mrs. Neville," she said helpfully. "We call her that because she looks like a cow."

I almost burst out laughing. Mrs. Neville *did* look like a cow. But Tabby looked bored.

I decided to also look bored. "I know," I said.

I sat with Tabby and Elizabeth every day for the rest of that week. And every day when Tabby was done not eating, we went down to the cloakroom where Tabby and I smoked and Elizabeth kept watch for Big Beef.

"Have you ever noticed about Beef?" Elizabeth said. "She wears shoes like nurses do, the ones with squishy bottoms so she can sneak up on you."

"Liz," said Tabby, "you're such a moodle."

Elizabeth beamed, like this was a compliment. And, judging from the way Tabby had just called her Liz, not Elizabeth, maybe it was.

"Liz" tickled Tabby under her chin and said she was a moodle, too. Tabby tickled her back.

I stood there feeling invisible.

It was Elizabeth who finally noticed. "It's a family thing," she explained for my benefit. "It goes back to when we were little. We call each other moodles all the time."

175

After that, I decided I needed to do something alone with Tabby, not something that involved Elizabeth, too. That day, at the end of school, I saw Tabby in the hallway leaning against her locker with a couple of her friends with their identically short skirts.

"Hey, Tabby," I said.

She didn't look too excited to see me.

"Who's that?" said one of her friends, a girl who had long blond hair like Tabby's and who I knew, from gym class, wore a black padded bra.

"Her?" Tabby said. "Margaret. She's new. She's a friend of Liz's."

"Meg," I said. "They have me listed as Margaret . . ."

"Whatever," the girl said.

Tabby flipped her hair over her shoulder with a flick of the wrist. And then she and the skirts walked away.

I spent the weekend doing three things: going online to see if Tabby was online, ignoring Elizabeth's IMs inviting me to sleep over, and looking in the mirror as I practiced the way Tabby flipped her hair over her shoulder.

On Monday before homeroom, I saw Tabby getting her stuff out of her locker. The skirts were nowhere to be seen, so I walked up and said hi.

She was too busy fishing through her locker for something to say hi.

"I have something for you," I said.

She looked at me like I was interesting for the first time.

"What is it?"

176

"Meet me in the cloakroom," I said. "Before lunch."

"But Liz . . ."

I dangled my purse in the air between us, signaling that whatever I had was in there.

"Okay," she said. "Before lunch."

Elizabeth pounced on me as soon as Spanish was over. "Don't you know how to IM?" she said.

"Everybody knows how to IM," I said.

"Well, you didn't answer my messages," she said. "I invited you to sleep over."

"I know," I said. Then I flipped my hair over my shoulder just the way I'd practiced and walked off to meet Tabby in the cloakroom.

Except that she wasn't there. I waited for five minutes, then five more, then, just to be sure, five more. I was about to leave, planning to spend the rest of the lunch period in a bathroom stall in case she and Elizabeth came down after Tabby was done not eating, but just as I stepped into the skinny passageway, I heard the faint squishing of rubber-soled footsteps coming in my direction. I ducked back into the cloakroom and flattened myself against the wall. I held my breath and listened. The footsteps stopped, then seemed to get quieter. Big Beef had evidently gone the other way.

Because of the Big Beef scare, I was late getting to Math. Which meant the only seat left was next to Elizabeth. She smiled her Lego smile at me, then pointed to the open page in her textbook.

"We're on question number three," she whispered.

I barely nodded.

"You feeling okay?" she said. "You weren't at lunch."

I said I was fine.

Elizabeth studied my face.

"You sure?" she said. "You don't look okay."

I pretended I didn't hear her.

I saw Tabby at her locker at the end of the day. I put on my too-cool-to-be-bothered face as I walked past to go to my locker, but as soon as she turned around and looked in my direction, I said hi instead.

"What's up?" She said this like she completely forgot that we were supposed to meet in the cloakroom, like she completely forgot I had something for her.

"Nothing." I tried to sound casual.

She started walking away.

"I still have that, you know, that thing for you," I said.

"You have something for me?" she said from behind her curtain of hair. "Oh, yeah."

"Don't worry," I said, even though Tabby didn't exactly look worried. "It's no big deal."

As soon as I said it was no big deal, her eyes drifted off to someone or something else down the hall.

"Well," I said quickly. "It's sort of a big deal, I guess. I mean, it's . . . it's . . ." I tried to think of the right word. From the foggy look in Tabby's eyes, I could tell she'd lost interest.

"It's unique," I said.

That got her attention. She checked her watch and said, "Okay, hurry up and give it to me. I have to be at my shrink's in twenty minutes."

I looked up and down the hall. "In the cloakroom," I said. "I can't show it to you here."

She blew on her bangs. "Okay," she said. "Just hurry up."

Being alone with Tabby in the cloakroom felt weird and different and not like I pictured it. Maybe it was because it was the end of the day, not lunchtime; maybe it was because it was just the two of us. Tabby blew on her bangs and looked bored, and for a minute I actually sort of wished Elizabeth was there with her Lego smile.

"So," said Tabby, "what is it?"

I reached inside my purse and pulled out a silver monogrammed lighter. It was my mom's. She didn't smoke anymore, but she kept it in a velvet bag in her jewelry box.

I handed it to Tabby.

She regarded it absentmindedly. Her face was blank.

"So what do you think?" I said.

She shrugged. "It's okay."

"It's engraved." I turned it over so Tabby could see the big cursive letter M engraved on the front. "See? It's unique."

Tabby frowned. "It's not that unique. If it had more than one letter — like a person's monogram — that would be unique."

I tried to think of something to make it better. "It was in the family."

She shrugged. "So you want to have a smoke?"

"Sure."

She pulled out her cigarettes and shook the box up and down. "There's only one left," she said.

I had opened my mouth to say she could have it when Tabby handed it to me. "We can share," she said.

179

I tried not to beam the way Elizabeth did. Tabby Lane had said "we," meaning me and her.

While Tabby threw the empty cigarette box in the trash, I put the cigarette between my lips. Tabby gave the lighter an expert flick. The lid flipped open with a satisfying *click*, but nothing happened. Tabby frowned. I swallowed.

"Try again," I said.

On the second try it worked. I inhaled quickly before the flame went out. Which meant I inhaled the fumes from the lighter fluid as well as a big gulp of smoke. Which meant I coughed and choked until tears were streaming down my face. I looked up to see Tabby's reaction.

She was laughing. It was the kind of laugh where someone's laughing with you, not at you. I knew the difference, so I laughed, too.

Which only made me cough harder.

Tabby thumped me lightly on the back.

Which meant I was coughing and laughing at the same time.

"Margaret," came a deep voice from behind me. "Perhaps you'd like to tell me what's so funny."

I turned around and came face-to-face with Big Beef.

I looked at the cigarette in my hand, then at Tabby. Her ice-blue eyes were wide with fear.

I thought about dropping the cigarette on the floor and grinding it out with my heel, but that would add destruction of school property to the crime. So I just stood there holding the evidence.

Finally, Big Beef sighed. "Ms. Lane," said Big Beef. "Would *you* like to tell me what's going on?"

Tabby's face brightened a little. And my heart filled with gratitude toward my new friend, Tabby Lane, of *the* Lanes. She'd get us out of this.

She knocked one clog against the other while she thought of what to say.

Finally she looked up at Big Beef, tossed her hair so that it fell in that perfectly random, perfectly perfect way.

"Margaret's new," she said.

I nodded, innocent.

"She's a friend of Elizabeth's."

"I see," said Big Beef.

I didn't see. But I figured Tabby knew what she was doing.

I shifted the burning cigarette to my other hand. Ashes fell on the floor.

"Please, Mrs. Neville . . ." Tabby gave her an angelic smile. "Don't be mad."

I also gave her what I hoped was an angelic smile.

Mrs. Neville sighed. "Smoking is a very serious offense," she said. "*You* know that, Tabby."

"I know," Tabby said sadly. She bit her lip and looked out from under her bangs shyly. She was the picture of remorse, a blond-haired angel in a plaid skirt. She looked over at me and smiled sadly. Then she turned to Mrs. Neville. "She was just trying to fit in."

I didn't get it. Who was just trying to fit in? Elizabeth?

Mrs. Neville folded her arms across her chest. "That's no excuse."

Mrs. Neville looked me up and down, stopping a minute to take in the still-burning cigarette in my hand. Then she turned to stare at Tabby — who was holding her hands behind her back.

"Tabby," said Mrs. Neville. "What do you have behind your back?"

Tabby's eyes went wide again. "Nothing," she said in a small voice.

"Let me see, then," said Mrs. Neville.

Tabby brought one pale, skinny arm out from behind her back and wiggled her empty fingers. She smiled shyly.

"The other hand . . . ," said Mrs. Neville.

Tabby looked like she was about to cry. I pictured how when this was over, I'd try to cheer her up, how I'd put my arm around her frail little shoulders and tell her not to worry, that we'd have fun being suspended, that we could go to the mall or to her house and read magazines and listen to music while everyone else was in school.

Her wide blue eyes darted back and forth between me and Mrs. Neville.

Finally, she withdrew the hand behind her back. She opened her palm to reveal the silver lighter.

Mrs. Neville shook her head sadly.

Tabby shook her head sadly, too, then stepped toward Mrs. Neville. "Margaret tried to give this to me," she said. "See? It's engraved. With the letter M."

I felt like I was falling all of a sudden, even though I was standing up. When I looked over at the two of them, they seemed to be standing far away from me.

Mrs. Neville sighed heavily. "I see," she said.

And all at once I saw, too. But I stood there and waited for Tabby to make it crystal clear.

"See?" she said again, sidling up to Mrs. Neville. "It's unique."

# THE BLANKET

### by Eddie de Oliveira

I'll tell you the thing I hate the most.

It is an inane, ignorant, and incorrect phrase that grownups — those who are supposed to know better — throw around casually. Every time I hear it, my face contorts itself into a deflating balloon. My frown goes south and begins to eat up everything below it, my eyes pop out of my head, and I twist my mouth and bite my lips. I cannot help it. I hate this phrase more than anything. More than cucumbers or minced meat. More than James "the Dick" Head, aggressive and gangly and who picks on everybody at school. More than football. More than Sundays.

"School days are the best days of your life."

That is the biggest heap of crap I have ever had the misfortune of hearing, and it is always said with such a smug "I-know-better-than-you" smirk.

I am thirteen years old, not tall, not short, and not amused. My favorite food is not pizza.

Kids at school call me emo. I call myself Luke.

I go to school, like every other kid in the world, because I have to. I do not understand when my parents and other grown-ups complain about their jobs. At least they are paid. I have to spend seven hours a day listening to bored, frustrated teachers driveling on when I know their minds are on other, more important things, and I don't get a penny.

The only good thing about school is that I cannot fall asleep there. I do not like going to bed anymore. Sleep has become the enemy. Sometimes I drink three cups of coffee and put on a really good DVD to keep me up. Sometimes I go to school after just half an hour of sleep the night before. I spend the whole day tired, and the next evening I sleep like twelve hours, which can be fine, but it can be awful. Because of the dream.

I do not understand the dream. It is stubborn, and scary, and so very strong. Last night was the third time in two weeks. I knew what would happen. It was always the same. Every time it is the same. It doesn't matter what has happened that day, or how happy I have been, for the dream is identical. But I still do not understand. This is not a nightmare. It is far worse than that. A nightmare ends when you wake up.

I see myself walking along a country road. The road is narrow, flanked by carefully trimmed hedges, behind which roll fields and fields of perfect green. It is a green so bright and precise that it looks computer-generated. The day is not overcast. Butterflies and dragonflies the size of small birds flit about carelessly. I am always wearing a black T-shirt, rather old, long, dark green shorts, and square, black sunglasses. I like the way I am dressed in the dream. I walk down the road, unsure of where I am going. The road is unfamiliar but it feels safe. It is summer, after all, and the sun brings happiness.

This picture of perfection lasts for a couple of minutes.

Then, quite suddenly, the blanket appears. I have learned to be fearful the minute I see myself in this dream, walking down the country road. I know the happiness is fake and temporary, and my sleeping self desperately tries to wake my dreaming self so that the blanket won't ruin everything. Because that's what it does. It ruins absolutely everything, sapping energy and converting joy into misery, peace into panic. It doesn't care. It shows no sympathy, no mercy, no remorse. I wish I could somehow wake up. But I know it is no use. And now, ever since I started having these dreams, I am deeply suspicious of any moment of happiness in my real life. Each and every time something very cool happens — like meeting a new friend, or a girl fancying me, or even just being told by a teacher that my essay is good — the feeling of pride, of excitement, of plain happiness is quickly followed by a weird, scared feeling. The dream has taught me never to trust something good, because, just like the beautiful, sunny walk down the country lane, it is bound to be replaced suddenly by something awful. I hate the fact that I can't trust happiness anymore.

This is the way the bliss is killed off in the dream: The country road becomes more and more narrow. The hedges on either side close in and grow taller, filled with messy weeds and ugly branches. Quite suddenly, they become too tall to jump over. No escape there. The sun dips snappily until it is on the verge of setting. The insects disappear. The day is not happy.

And there it is. There it always is. About fifty meters behind me, lurking in the road, waiting to give chase. It is a blanket. But no ordinary blanket this. Standing about ten feet tall and five feet wide, it is jet-black and five inches thick. The blanket moves of its own accord. It has no legs, but it can run. It has no

185

brain, but it is sharp and knows what it is doing. The blanket begins its chase.

I feel my heart beating quicker and quicker. I begin to run. Occasionally I turn around to catch a glimpse, and that just makes me even sadder, even more scared, because the blanket is always gaining ground on me. I run faster. The blanket, billowing as it runs, is slowly catching up. My heart feels as though it is about to burst out of my chest. I begin sweating. This is the only moment my sleeping self and dream self share a physical feeling of panic; I always wake up from these dreams with my T-shirt soaked right through. As fast as I run, the blanket still gets nearer.

It is always the same. I know I cannot defeat the vile blanket. But somehow, somewhere inside of me I hold on to a faint, feeble hope that if I could just run a little bit faster, or find a tiny hole in the hedge, or bump into another person wandering down the country road, if I could just discover one of those salvations, then I could defeat the bastard blanket.

The dream is cruel. One time, I saw a gap in the hedge on the other side of the road. I raced over to it, aware of the blanket creeping closer. But the closer I got, the smaller the gap became, until I came right up to the hedge and there was no hole whatsoever. No escape route. As if the blanket chase wasn't bad enough, this glimpse of safety was just a vicious tease.

Other nights, it wasn't a hole in the hedge that offered hope. It was the strange sense that I was about to wake up. I could feel myself trying desperately to break out of the sleep. Somehow I could see myself lying on my bed and was trying to wake myself up. Very strange. But very frustrating, because I just couldn't snap out of my slumber.

As I sense the blanket getting nearer, I can feel my body tensing up and clasping on to the mattress.

It is no good. It is never any good.

I am still running. Then I always turn around one last time. This is the moment I dread more than any other in the dream. I can hear my sleeping self whining as I try so desperately to wake up, to avoid this horrible moment. It feels a bit like I am being suffocated, or stuck in a confined prison cell unable to even stretch my arms. I feel so small and so scared and I can't wake up. I can't wake up.

And then it happens.

It always happens. The blanket dives on me, cloaking my back, wrapping itself around my legs, embracing me with its coldness and its incredible weight. It behaves like an octopus, its tentacles gripping tight all over my body, almost crushing my rib cage, restricting my breathing, weighing down on my back so heavily that it feels as though I am carrying a rucksack full of rocks.

And that is that. I can walk, but slowly. The blanket makes me lethargic, snoozy, and dislocated. Yes, that's it — dislocated. Like I am in the world but not, at the same time. Like I am out of my body but still functioning within it. Does that make any sense? Because it doesn't to me, but I know how real it feels, and how powerful it is, and how frightened I am each time the blanket covers me. I feel alone, like the only person for miles. It makes me sad, and I still cannot see why, even though I've had these dreams for three months now. But above all, it makes me scared.

I decided to call the blanket The Fear. Even after I wake from my nightmare, The Fear sticks around, sometimes for weeks. As much as I dread sleep, I sometimes sleep for so long — as much as twelve hours a night. Some nights, The Fear is in my dream, other times it's not. Some days I have come home from school, eaten my tea, and gone straight to sleep. But no matter how much I sleep, I always feel the same — so tired, so lazy, so not in the mood for anything very much. My best friend, Nick, does not understand, but I don't blame him. I don't call him up or return his calls, and he gets upset, but I can't really explain myself and that makes him angry. Then I feel worse about myself for being so bad about getting in touch. When The Fear comes along, I become stuck in a vicious and hideous circle; I distance myself from Nick, feel bad for doing so, and then feel sadder when I find out how sad he feels about it. Nick always hangs around though. He is very good to me, even though sometimes I am very bad to him. I can't help it. I don't want to be, but The Fear just takes a hold and the very thought of being sociable and chatty scares me.

My mum is worried. My dad doesn't notice any difference. Dads never do. Mum is too scared to talk about it directly, but she keeps asking if I am all right and if the other kids at school are bothering me. She doesn't like it when I skip dinner or when I sleep so long. She has started reading books about growing up by doctors with long, German-looking names and lots of letters after their names. I don't really know how to answer her when she asks me all the questions. I do not want her to send me to a doctor.

I wish so hard that I could shake it.

On my thirteenth birthday, I have a small party with friends. My mum buys the best cake I've ever had. It's sponge, with jam and cream, delicious icing, and *Happy Birthday Luke* with the *Luke* written on a trippy orange cloud. She puts thirteen candles on it.

In previous years when I blew out my birthday candles, I would wish for silly things like a special present, or that I would live forever, or that this girl with really long, dark red hair called Maggie would like me. But this time I have a really strong feeling come over me before I blow out the candles. I know I need to have this wish, because this could be a chance to make the impossible possible.

I wish that The Fear would disappear.

But I don't have much hope. Ever since I was five and wished for the BMX bike that never came, I've known that what you wish for when you blow your candles out is never what you get.

# THE WAITRESS

### by Matthue Roth

My head slammed against the locker door.

The fist that was currently attached to my head, its nails digging into my hair, turned ninety degrees to the right. My head turned along with it. I gave a short moan, more from instinct than protest. The locker's air grates dug into my eye, and I squelched it shut, just as a precautionary measure. *Jupiter Jason Glazer*, I told myself, *you have got to find a better way to make new school friends.*

"Like I said," said the mouth that the aforementioned fist was attached to, "you went and got real lucky. This new locker of yours is prime real estate. So I guess *your* locker is *our* locker now, right?"

Somewhere behind him, a crony belched up a laugh.

I decided that the path of least resistance would be to simply agree. Although my shoulder blades were currently at angles I didn't think were possible, I did my best attempt to shrug them in a display of broadcasted compliance.

"Okay," I chirped amicably.

I just need to tell you: I'm not new at this.

I'm new to this school, this neighborhood, this life. I was

born in Zvrackova, a city in Russia so small even its suburbs had never heard of it. That was before my parents threw me in a suitcase, got on a plane, and relocated our family to the Yards.

And, in my fourteen years of life on this planet Earth, spanning two continents, ten thousand miles, and countless school bullies, there is one thing I have learned: When two hundred pounds of man flesh comes at you with an attitude and an agenda, that is the ideal moment to start adjusting your point of view. Especially when that two hundred pounds is shrouded in a T-shirt formerly owned, according to its insignia, by a band called the Thrill Kill Kult, with fists garnished by two (allowed in school, but only barely) bracelets studded with metal spikes, a (definitely, totally not allowed anywhere near school property) metal spike collar, and a goatee slicked with enough oil and hair gel to render it as sharp, pointy, and lethal as any knife he could have smuggled in.

So, yeah. In the moment, agreeing with him did not seem like a bad idea at all.

Bates was so surprised, he let go of my head immediately. "What did you just say?" he demanded, a surprised roar that sounded like a lion accidentally swallowing a small frog.

I chose that moment to enact my denouement.

I ducked beneath the arch framed by the bodies of Harris Bates — the owner of the fist — and his best friends-slash-sidekicks, Nail and Lauren, the pillars of said arch. Between them, there was enough steel on their clothes and in their bodies to set off the school metal detectors two floors away.

I dived between their bodies and onto the floor, skidding an elbow on the linoleum. I slid to a stop, hopped up, and leaped straight into a run.

191

They exchanged glances, which turned into slow, evil smiles. Then they started after me, foot darting over foot, one after the other.

My first steps were clumsy stumbles. In seconds, they had turned into a full galloping run.

I shot down the basement corridor, feeling the sudden slap of recycled air against my face. My chin-length hair beat in my eyes, then fell as I gained speed. The hall flew by in a blur of You-Can-Do-It posters featuring cute animals and rock stars that hadn't been cool for at least seven years. I feinted to the left, then dove right, dodging the girls' tennis team, who had chosen that moment to congregate in the hall and talk about the championships, or the captain's date last weekend, or something else to do with scoring.

Then I felt the tiny, sharp pull of an inhumanly small hand affixing itself to my forearm.

I spun around, finding myself face-to-face with a girl in a soccer team uniform. "Hey," she said. "Are you the guy that Bates is chasing?"

"What?" I glanced back over my shoulder. Bates and his compatriots were standing in the main doors of the hallway, looking left and right like hungry predators in the midst of a hunt. "Oh, er . . . yeah. That might be me."

"Then get in here. We can hide you; he's an asshole."

Her hand still on the scruff of my collar, she threw me down and into the crowd. I crouched low, my knees digging into the linoleum floor. I looked up at the girl, flashing her a quick smile of thanks. She scowled down at me and, the next thing I knew, I felt a sharp crack on the back of my head.

After that, I didn't pick my head up for a while.

For a second — just a second, I swear — I'd caught a glimpse below her skirt. She was wearing standard white underwear, slight traces of a lace pattern on the edge where it met her thigh — but nothing like what I had imagined girls' underwear to be like. Panties.

Guilt began welling up in my head. I wondered if she was feeling violated. I wondered if she realized it was an accident.

And then I realized: Right now, I was surrounded by girls in miniskirts. And their legs were all at the level of my eye. I had never looked at porn, but it was like some bizarre dream that's about sex but isn't sexy at all: a solid, unbreakable fortress of girls' legs, every shade of the spectrum from postsummer tan to solid black, quivering and twittering in time with the uninterrupted giggles of gossip that came from above. "No *way*, really?" one girl said, as her legs crossed, hugging each other around the knees. I tried to listen harder, as if, now that I was a foreigner in jock girls' country, I should maybe learn the language.

But, no. After a few minutes had passed, my original savior yanked me up, wrapping her skinny, scrawny fingers around my skinny, scrawny arm.

"They're gone," she whispered.

As I stood, still looking around to calm my red-alerting nerves, their conversation seemed to fizzle out. The girls started looking at me. It seemed like, for the first time, everyone else had noticed that they were currently acting as my firewall. And they did not look happy to be doing it. The bell rang and, like a ring of dancers in a Broadway show, the circle dispersed, each girl scuttering off in a different direction to her respective class.

God. I hadn't even opened up my mouth.

I hadn't even *met* them. They'd barely seen my face long enough to decide whether I was ugly or not. How did they already know to write me off as a nerd? What is the invisible secret mark that makes popular kids so intrinsically recognizable to their equals, and makes them rope off the rest of us into the dim and dreary purgatory of normality?

The rest of the day didn't go much better. My bio teacher thought that Jupiter was a girl's name, my Spanish teacher tried to pronounce my name in Spanish, and my English teacher couldn't find my name on the roll and insisted that I wasn't actually registered to go to school here. Just as she was about to send me to the principal's office for rerouting or deportation or something even more sinister, I told her to let *me* have a look at it, grabbed the roll book out of her hand, and found myself listed under J for *Jupiter, Glazer* instead of G for *Glazer, Jupiter*. I guess I said it a little more aggressively than I absolutely needed to. From behind me — and I was standing right in front of the classroom, at the teacher's desk — I heard someone go "*daaaamn*," a low whistle, then a murmur spreading among my fellow students.

The corners of my teacher's mouth twitched, much like a natural predator sniffing out the direction of its dinner. From the back of the room, Tonya Murray and Vanessa Greyscole and all the not-ready-for-prime-time sorority girls made sounds like stuck noses, just aching to laugh out loud at me.

That night, to celebrate my allegedly victorious first day of school, my parents took me to the same place we went to celebrate virtually every family birthday, anniversary, and good report card ever — the Country Club Diner. In honor of the occasion, I wore a dress shirt with a collar. I had to try on all three collared shirts in my closet before I found one to cover the bruises that Bates had put there, but finally I looked presentable enough to cover myself.

The Country Club is the most revered and upscale deep-fried, oil-hanging-in-the-air, waitresses-who-call-you-"hon" place you can imagine. They even have a dress code there. It runs along the lines of No Shirt, No Service, but it *is* a dress code.

We waited in the lobby, which smelled of cheap powdery mints and cigarettes, but not unpleasantly. I hate cigarettes with a passion — at my old school, my old best friend Garfinkel had stopped talking to me because I wasn't cool enough on the same day that he started smoking cigarettes — but I actually really, really like the smell of cigarette-inflicted lobbies. Maybe it just feels poetic. Maybe it's dirtiness and nostalgia all lumped together, although nostalgia for what?

Finally, a waitress called our names and escorted us to our booth.

Most of the waitresses around us were totally creepy, old ladies with hunchbacks and fake hair that stood up in a messily asymmetrical beehive and would still be standing after a nuclear explosion, smelling of Lysol as they pointed out the daily specials on your menu with hook-nails over your shoulder.

Our waitress must have been the youngest there by about sixty-five years.

She looked to be most of the way through high school, three or four years older than me. She had high cheekbones, longish blond hair bound up in a knot at the back, and a small nose that turned up at the end. Her eyes were distant and vacant, like she'd been watching TV for hours, or maybe just working at a job that she longed to be rescued from. Right then and there, I felt a sudden injection of a fantasy whereupon I grabbed her hand, she ripped off the clip-on maroon bowtie and yanked the matching vest right over her head, and we ran out through the kitchen, took the first bus out of the Yards, and spent all night downtown, watching independent movies and drinking Italian espresso-based drinks that no one in the Yards had a hope of pronouncing correctly.

This fantasy tumbled apart the minute she opened her mouth.

"Ya want drinks now or just warter ta start wit?" she said.

Her voice was pure Yards, words running into each other like caramel, totally unmodulated. She sounded like every Yards girl did, a cross between a fifties B-movie gangster and a robot. When she stopped talking, her mouth kept moving, and her rear teeth cracked a stick of gum so emphatically that my father winced in his seat.

My mother, a.k.a. the most neurotic person on earth, was already scrubbing soup stains off the laminated menu pages with her napkin. "Can you tell me, which specials are for tonight?" she asked, her not-used-to-English voice making static bumps out of the language I'd worked so hard to get smooth. I sank a little lower in my chair.

"They're on tha first page," said our waitress, still hovering rigidly in front of our table, pen and ordering pad poised in the air.

I wondered if she was just putting on the accent as a front, if she, too, had learned to blend in with the crowds. I wondered

196

whether if we found ourselves alone together she would slip out of her accent like bad camouflage, whisper in my ear like a perfect American, crisp ennunciation like a late-night anchor on the TV news.

Totally on instinct, subconsciously, I looked over at her chest. She was wearing a bleached cardboard name tag, also laminated. Beside the Country Club Diner logo it said, in all capital letters, MARGIE.

My mother folded the menu shut, as if to demonstrate her remarkable ability of instant memorization. "I will have the tuna salad grinder," she announced to MARGIE, whose facial expression was growing more bored by the minute.

Without waiting for me and my father to order, MARGIE snapped her pad shut. "I'll be right out with your warters," she announced to us. "Youse can order then if ya want."

For some reason, I really wanted a Coke. Someone at the next table over had ordered one, and the way the ice cracked in the glass, the way the bubbles fought each other sizzling to the top, it looked suddenly really appetizing. But there was this unspoken rule in our family, everyone only drank water at a restaurant. Partly this was because they always charged as much for a glass in restaurants as stores did for a two-liter bottle. The other half of it — at least, on my part — was that my parents had just invested all their money into the factory, the block-long warehouse inside which we now lived.

So, yeah, going out to a restaurant like this — sitting at a table that didn't used to be a conveyor belt, drinking out of glasses that weren't stained with factory dust, that anonymous soot that seems to come from everywhere and gets into all your clothes and food — even though our lavish dinner out was at a cheap diner that didn't look anything like a country club, we were, in our own way, eating like kings.

I watched my father sip his water, taking great care to avoid brushing the ice cubes with his mustache. My mother was spending an inordinate amount of time adjusting the napkin (cloth!) to drape perfectly on her lap. I picked up my own glass of water, ran the tips of my fingers over the raised bumps of the meniscus, and realized that MARGIE was staring at me, waiting.

"Sir?"

Her voice was absolutely flat. I couldn't tell if she was making fun of me or not.

"Uh," I fumbled. The menu was open to the page of steaks. The words swam over my eyes, each sounding more barbaric than the last: sirloin, pink, rib-eye. Did people really eat rib-eye steaks? Were they made of real eyes?

"Omelette," I said, taking a sudden urge and running with it. "Spinach, tomatoes, and cheddar cheese, with hash browns, grilled hot and hard, extra paprika, and rye toast."

Her pencil scribbled fast to keep up with my order. When at last she had finished, she glanced up from her pad, flashed me a single, lasting, cold stare — the kind that pretty girls with long blond hair are wont to direct at miscreant boys such as myself — and vanished into the kitchen.

"An omelette?" said my mother. "With eggs? This is what you get for dinner at a restaurant? I could make you omelette at home, for nothing."

"Is fine." My father was already starting to defend me. He grabbed my wrist, shaking it like I'd just won an Olympic trophy. "Tonight is his honor dinner. Jupiter can make his own choice of anything he want."

The waitress tapped her pen impatiently on the pad. She was smirking at me, as if to say, *You're fourteen years old and you still go out to dinner with your parents?*

I looked around at the rest of the restaurant. Old people in khaki shorts and sandals. A family with several children gathered at a round table in the center of the room, the parents impossibly young. They were both huge — fat, yes, but also *huge*, squeezed into their skin. Their haircuts and clothes were hopelessly Yards, either way out of date or stuck in a timeless Kmart vortex. The husband and wife almost looked the same, dressed in their sloppy T-shirts, with four or five kids that looked identical, or almost identical. They were all about the same height, and they all had dirty blond hair. They didn't look more than a couple years older than me, that couple — *that* was the scary part. I wondered if that was going to be my future straight out of high school: a potbelly and a family of indistinct-looking kids. There was another family in the restaurant that was clearly Russian — you could tell. The parents didn't look American at all, and the kids looked way *too* American. Cheap button-down shirts and single-sheet pattern dresses for the adults, backward caps, sport-team jackets, and skanky skirts for the girls. Lots of visible electronics. Cell phones clipped to the belt, pagers in abundance, and, for some reason, sunglasses that made them look like junior Mafia. And this excessively Christian family, all with mop-top haircuts and prescription eyeglasses and posture that they learned out of a book, stealing nervous glances like they were constantly consciously thinking that everyone else in here was going to pounce on them at once and start punching them and chasing them straight to hell.

It was absolutely true. I was probably the only fourteen-year-old boy in America who was going out with his parents after the first day of school. The soccer team girls were probably all out on dates with their boyfriends tonight. Even Bates was probably out with Lauren or some other heavy-metal girl, doing God knows what in a dark basement somewhere.

All these families were clustered in a restaurant named after an American institution that none of us would ever have a shot at getting into. It was like all of my prospective futures had lined themselves up in front of me, and none of them looked like something I wanted to grow up to be. Man, the first day of school was in my body like the flu. I needed to get out of there.

"I'll be right back." I was standing up, eyes grazing the place, looking for a bathroom. Without really knowing where I was going, I stood up and shot off.

Going to the bathroom in a new place is one of my favorite things. I know it sounds gross, but bathrooms, when you're my age, are the only bona fide places where you can hide out from your parents. Every place I go with my parents, sooner or later, I need to escape from them and hide out. And each place I hide out, every bathroom, is different. Some are sleazy, with cigarette butts all over the floor, leftover pee bubbling in the urinals. Others are clean, almost eerily hygienic — so much so that you begin to suspect the staff of hiding out in there, making sure nobody does anything too gross or permanent. But the best thing about bathrooms, really, is the graffiti. Everything from the trite-but-funny "Here I sit/brokenhearted/come to shit/but only farted" to ruminations on the universe, to those almost-possibly-real girls' names and phone numbers written on the

200

walls, either by vengeful ex-boyfriends or (please God please) by the girls themselves, curious to see what kind of teenage boys are reading them.

I followed a hunch and slipped into the hallway next to the kitchen.

MARGIE was standing there, right in the doorway, staring at her nails. She looked both utterly fascinated and utterly bored. Her eyes were wide, and it seemed to convey a degree of depth that had been absent from her previous dealings at our dinner table.

"Hey," I said.

"Yeah?"

She looked up from her nails.

I took one hand out of my pocket, gave her a little wave.

"Whaddyawant?"

I counted the words in my head. *What. Do. You. Want.* Four words, and she'd managed to condense them into a single, polysyllabic word, with no breathing space at all in between. There must be a Nobel Prize category for that.

"Uh, I was actually just looking for . . ." I said slowly, half-way into my sentence before I realized I was going to ask for the bathroom. *Bathroom.* There had to be a better word for it. Or, at the very least, a word you could use with girls. Facilities? Lavatory? In a flash, simplicity seemed like the coolest response, and before I could check myself I'd finished my sentence, ". . . the boys' room?"

Shit.

She didn't even blink. "Right over there," she said, nodding behind me.

I looked over my shoulder. There, on bright red plastic signs, were two silhouettes, the international symbols for *I need to go NOW.*

I blinked at her, briefly, coolly, as if to thank her without further sacrificing my integrity, and turned to follow her nod.

"Hey, wait." She tugged on my sleeve. I wasn't out of this yet.

"Yeah?" I spun around carefully, making sure she didn't let go of my shoulder.

"You look sorta farmiliar," she said. "Do ya go ta Yardley?"

Nathan Yardley High, the high school that mostly everyone in the Yards went to, was just down the street. There were about three thousand kids there, bussed in from all over the Yards. Everyone from my class would be going there next year. I couldn't say yes, and I really, really didn't want to say no.

"No," I said, struck with a sudden inspiration. "I'm at North Shore, it's this special-admissions high school downtown —"

"Wow," she said — still in that android monotone, but her eyes opened in newfound appreciation. "You must be pretty smart or somethin', huh?"

I shrugged. If I was playing the part of a North Shore kid, I might as well do away with the false modesty.

"Hey — I got to take my cigarette break now, or I don't get another one for an hour. You wanna come?" She nodded toward the door marked EXIT, which was right next to the door marked GENTLEMEN.

And then she threw me instead into the broom closet, shut the door behind her, inserted a single, long-nailed finger into the collar of her dress shirt, and yanked it down so that the shirt ripped in half, buttons flying everywhere, her lacy-bra'd breasts popping out like a cuckoo clock, like a pair of grenades, with me at ground zero. Her hair got in her face. Her hair got in my face. Our tongues dove into each other like crazed monkeys battling, fingers grabbed fingers, pulling into our flesh, trying to force our bodies even closer together. Her skin was white and smooth, like new, just-out-of-the-package soap. Her lips were thin and crisp, like a promotional letter opener just out of the plastic wrapping. I tried to pull myself away, then relented, pressing my torso against her, hoping against everything that she noticed, that she could smell how incredibly much I wanted her.

Oh my God. I am a teenage boy. I am loquaciously, dis-*gust*ingly horny. I am horny for anything that moves. I have fantasies about the girls on the 9:00 sitcoms, girls on the 10:00 dramas, and the girls in the deodorant and car commercials in between. My head is in the gutter, and the rest of my body is squeezed underneath it.

We stood right outside the exit door, a few steps away from the kitchen, and she pulled on the hoodie she'd brought out with her. It was tight. It pulled in her stomach and silhouetted her breasts a lot more clearly than the loose shirt and vest of her uniform. She drew a lighter and a pack of cigarettes out of the pocket and lit one up, barely looking at me as she drew the flame in with a deep breath. Her hair bristled. It looked nice.

"So," she said. She looked at me expectantly, like my being here was a privilege, and now I had to earn it.

"So," I echoed, not sure what to say. I folded my hands in front of my belt, realized I was standing with the posture of a fifty-year-old college professor, and quickly slid them into my back pockets. "You live around here?"

"Yeah," she grunted. When she talked, the smoke curled

out in small flames, like a dragon's breath. "My parents got an apartment a few blocks away. I'm saving up so I can move out of that shithole and get my own place, probably another shithole. But at least it'll be my shithole. Do you?"

"Yeah, kinda. Down where Yardley Ave stops being a hill and flattens out, over near the docks."

"Oh yeah?" she asked, taking a deep, impressed toke. "Rough neighborhood."

"Parts of it are. You learn to lay low."

"I had a boyfriend who ran DVD players for these guys, he was down there all the time. They kept them in one of those old warehouses, not even locked. You could just walk right in and help yourself. There ain't too many houses around there, are there?"

I shrugged noncommittally, trying to cover up for when she'd talked about having a boyfriend and I'd winced. "There's a few. It seems rough, but it's mostly quiet."

"Man. That's not too bad. I bet I could rent a whole house around there for what an apartment would cost. That would be pretty tight. I could even have friends move in — of course, I wouldn't, that would kill the whole purpose of it. Hey, are there any houses around there up for rent now, do you know?"

"I dunno. I'm kind of, you know, taken care of."

"Still doing the parental thing, huh?"

She said "the parental thing" as if it was an extreme improbability that any child above the age of teething would ever live with his parents. Not sure how to reply to that, I played it cool. "They're not so bad," I said, offering up an indifferent shrug. "Mostly we live in two different worlds. I think in English, and they think in some other language."

"Yeah, well, you don't *sound* like you think in English."

I didn't say anything, not sure whether I should be offended or not.

Other things about me that I was insecure about, I could hide. My accent stuck out like a bad hair day without a hat, like a zit that never went away. My hair was fuzzy, big curls sprinting out in a Sideshow Bob 'do that required refreshingly little effort. She ruffled the top of it now, as if petting a puppy. "Don't knock it. You're cute. And then you open your mouth and that voice comes out, that voice of yours, and it doesn't sound anything like you expect it to. I bet you're good at throwing people for a loop, yeah?"

"I'm all right," I said noncommittally.

"Nice. So what's with the accent anyway?"

"What's with it? I'm with it, I guess."

"Heh," she laughed. She laughed in a way that sounded like she'd contemplated what she was laughing at, thought about it for a while, and still didn't think it was funny. "If you were really swift, you'd say, 'What accent?'"

I didn't reply. Now I was listening to her own voice, how much softer and less abrasive it had gotten since we'd been out here. "How about you, then?" I said. "Now, you barely sound like you're from the Yards at all."

"Yeah, I dunno," she said. The gravellyness crept in, but only slightly. Maybe only because she was thinking about it now. "It's a defense mechanism, you know? You got to communicate with people on their level. You got to make sure they don't give you shit."

I waited.

For a moment, it seemed like she was in another world.

205

Like there was something in her voice that she wasn't saying. Then she snapped out of it and snapped back to looking at me. She lay a hand on my chest. I felt like I should leap back, like she'd just bumped into me — it was so direct and so forward and even, if only inside my brain, so sexual. Her nail was right over my nipple. Her palm was hot, and I wondered if she was going to pull me into her for a kiss.

Instead, she let go. She stepped back like nothing had just happened.

"But, come on," she said, laying one hand on a hip, cocking a posture like she was examining me from afar again. "What's the deal with your accent? Are you an android, or is your larynx just on steroids?"

I gulped. "It's Russian. My parents are from Russia. We got airlifted out of the country when I was seven."

"Oh yeah? How was that for you?"

"I don't remember. Only thing I remember is, my parents woke me up early one morning, then they made me stuff all the clothes in my room inside a duffel bag in, like, ten minutes. They said to just bring the important clothes — they were too busy, they couldn't even help me — and, when they unpacked, they discovered I had only brought my holiday dress suit and a shit-load of underwear. Oh, and a black market copy of *Where the Wild Things Are*, which was my favorite book at the time. Anyway, they hustled me out the door, to a plane. I stayed up the whole plane flight, gazing out the window, and fell asleep as soon as we landed. I woke up a few hours later, we were in this rusty recycled car, headed for the Yards, and then I turned into an American."

She barked out a bitter, dry laugh. "Damn, dude," she said.

"I think that's the first time I ever heard the Yards being a happy ending."

"Well, damn yourself," I said, trying to project the sauciness into my voice. "I didn't think I was up to the ending yet."

She smiled.

For the first time, it seemed like I'd found something soft about her. Her voice, her chin, her eyes, even her breasts were so perfect, ample and fleshed-out, plentiful in the way of Italian mothers and collagen patients, but perfect in the other sense of that word, too, stiff as a Renaissance picture. From her body, and from her attitude, as well, she was the total opposite of me: totally composed, totally on top of her own social scene, and totally in control.

But, man, when she cracked her mouth open and let her smile poke through — awash in all her thin-lipped glory, crooked teeth swimming inside, gums the pale pink of someone who runs their toothbrush under the water instead of scrubbing their teeth at night — it was so imperfect and asymmetrical, so flawed and honest, that it actually made her look beautiful. I wanted to take that smile in my pocket and fall asleep with it under my pillow, to have it keep me warm through the cold of the warehouse night.

"And it isn't so happy, either," I said.

She opened her mouth and looked at me — *what do you mean?* — in the way that perfect people always do, those girls who say whatever they want and expect everyone else to love them for it. But then she closed her mouth, as if to take back that sentiment, and instead she reached over with those intense fingernails and pulled my collar down.

I winced, seeing her see my battle scars. She looked grossed out, as any normal person would, but not revolted.

By which I mean, she didn't flinch. And she didn't look like she was going anywhere.

"Yeah, well, you know what?" she said. "It's gonna be. After what we go through to get where we are, it better be happy. It better fucking be."

She brushed aside one permed curl from her forehead. I could see purple skin of her own beneath it, a nasty contusion that ran along most of her scalp.

And, at that moment, I was about to offer her a room in our warehouse. I was about to tell her, forget about my hormones, forget about getting an apartment of your own, I'll take you away from all this.

She reached down, ground the cigarette out on the heel of her shoe, and tossed the butt in the half-cranked-up window of someone's car.

I waited for her to say something, and then I realized that she was staring at me. Probably because I was staring at her leg, long and pale and enclosed in a showcase of nude-colored fishnets, still exposed in the air after the grinding of her cigarette.

She grinned at me and ruffled my hair again. When she spoke again, it was like her accent had switched back on. Like everything that had just happened between us didn't actually happen.

"Look, I gotta go back inside," she said. "Guess you do, too. Anyway, good luck and stuff. It was good talking with you."

"Well, hey, thanks yourself," I said. "And hope to see you around, Margie."

"Margie? Oh, jeez, that's not me — I just forgot to bring my name tag. I'm only Margie for tonight."

I watched her climb the stairs, still in the parking lot, still stuck inside the memory of her legs. Her legs and her head. I watched as she hesitated for a moment on the precipice between the last step and the door inside, as if she was trying to decide whether she was going back in or not.

And then she did, and then I remembered, I had a life to get back to, too.

# THE BIRDS OF FLEMING PARK

## by Kevin Waltman

Every fall the birds here lose their minds. They stop here for a month before migrating farther south, and our town has tried all kinds of strategies — amplified bird calls at night, sculptures of fake hawks to scare them off — to no avail. Their favorite targets are downtown at the courthouse, where they perch in hordes on the limestone edges, purple and white polka dots speckling the stairs beneath them, and Fleming Park, where they get so loud that families half a mile away are forced to use earplugs or white noise to drown them out.

"It's like something out of Hitchcock," my art teacher, Mr. Poole, said last week.

"Not exactly," I said.

"I'm talking about Alfred Hitchcock, Benny. He wrote *The Birds*. I'm sorry if my allusions are a little outdated for you."

"It's not that, Mr. Poole."

"Then what?"

"*The Birds* was an early sixties film, and it was symbolic of the violence humans inflict on nature, but in the film the birds fight back. Our problem is that we're too kind to the birds. I mean, we could poison them or shoot them, but that would upset some people's sensibilities. So we let them crap all over us. And that's not like the Hitchcock film at all."

I heard a few girls in the room laugh, and Mr. Poole sighed and put his hands on his hips, not even aware that he was dabbing his jeans with oil paint. Mr. Poole is an old hippie who still can't believe that he wound up teaching high school art in Indiana instead of giving celebrated art shows. His revolution never came, and rather than being the artist sipping brandy in the corner, looking eccentric, he is just our weird art teacher with red smudges near his fly.

"Is that it, Benny?"

"And, technically, Hitchcock didn't write the film," I added. "He directed it."

Crimson gathered at his collar and shot in little sprouts up his neck. He sent me to the principal. Nothing new.

I usually go to Fleming Park, across the street from our house, to read before the light fades for the day. I might be the only person left in town who isn't bothered by the birds. In fact, their noise is so constant in the park, you can begin to forget it after a while, or at least I can once I get locked in on reading. I could go home, but my father and brother are always in front of the television, eating fast food, and some days I can't even bear to watch them — shrieking birds I can stand; family watching the tube, I can't. I have a little stash of books, even a bottle of booze smuggled from my father's cabinet. Ollie, my younger brother, used to come with me when we were kids, and we imagined our little hideaway as something fantastic — an elaborate bomb shelter or a military headquarters, the two of us survivors of terrific disasters, but with all the amenities we'd ever need. Of

211

course, now Oliver spends all his time in front of the television, and I can see our old shelter for what it is: two large slabs of soggy plywood propped up on stacks of cinder blocks we stole from a construction site, all of it covered by branches and vines and a green tarp riddled with holes. That's it — a pretty humble place, and one that smells more and more like urine and mold. That's the price of growing up: Things merely are what they are.

In the fall, as the birds spike in population, the park users dwindle and I am out here alone most of the time. The day after my argument with Mr. Poole, though, I saw a man in a trench coat walking with his head down, murmuring now and then. He'd walk a few paces, then stop to kneel down, press his thumb into the mud, and lift it to his nose. He'd walk a few more paces, dig in his pockets, wipe some gel on his finger, and smear it on the ground. His hair stood up in patches and his shoes looked like they'd been chewed by dogs. At first I thought he was some criminal scouting places to take his victims, but he looked too casual, like he had nothing that sinister to hide. He kept coming closer to my hideout, going through his ritual — walk, kneel, press, lift, walk, dig, wipe, smear — every minute or so. His approach made me nervous, because crazy is crazy even in a small town like ours. I didn't know whether to hide, run, or call out to him so he'd know I was there.

He was about ten yards away, so close I could hear the fabric of his ragged coat swishing when he walked, when I finally decided to call out.

"Hey," I said, and he jumped like a firecracker, crumbs and change and little vials spilling from his pockets. He fumbled for a moment, tangled in his trench coat, and when he stood back up there was mud stuck in his short, gray beard.

"I didn't mean to scare you," I said, still ready to run if he started after me.

"You might not have meant to," he said, voice shaking as he picked wet leaves off his coat, "but I'll be darned if my heart isn't about to explode."

He looked at me, eyes wide, and his trench coat fell open so I could see his T-shirt, a picture of a bald eagle on it with the caption *GREAT AMERICAN BIRD LOVER*. I couldn't help laughing at that, and soon the bird lover laughed, too, even though he was rubbing his elbow in pain. He introduced himself as Rudolph Whitaker, but instead of shaking my hand he stroked his beard, looking at me like I was the dubious one.

"So what the hell are you doing out here?" I asked.

"It's hard to explain." He looked around, his eyes keen on a nest in a nearby tree.

"Try me."

"I'm here to solve the bird problem."

"Oh, the bird guy," I said. "The bird talker. I read about you in the paper."

"The Bird Whisperer," he corrected, then looked down as if embarrassed by the name. The newspaper had run an article on him that weekend, calling him the Bird Whisperer, a lame reference to a lame movie. Of course, the newspaper wasn't even original in its mediocrity, as he had been so dubbed by a slate of midwestern towns with similar bird problems. "But that's good that a kid your age reads the newspaper. Shows inquisitiveness."

"Or boredom," I said. "So what's your scam?"

"There's no scam."

"Sure. You get these towns to pay you all kinds of money to take care of their bird problems, but you say you don't hurt them. It's all PETA-friendly and everything."

He had stopped laughing, more insulted by my accusation than he had been injured by his fall. "Excuse me," he said.

He walked off through the shade of the trees, repeating his routine. One time he looked back at me, as if inviting me to follow along and inspect his work, but I cracked open a book and pretended to read, eyeing him over the edge until he was gone.

I had the house to myself for a few minutes when I got home. In fact, our house was becoming so lonesome that I thought maybe I wouldn't need to go to Fleming Park much anymore. But then Ollie came in, tracking mud across the linoleum and carpet, and he immediately turned on the television at high volume. All that I could have blocked out, but then he lifted up his shirt and pulled out a dirty magazine and started thumbing through it.

"Put that away," I said.

"It's Dad's," he replied, as if that was justification. "I found it in his room."

"Don't you see that porn is fantasy? It's so unhealthy, almost as bad as that freaking television you've got yammering at you all the time. It objectifies women and, because they're so used to imaginary sexuality, it desensitizes men to actual women." I sat back down with my book, deciding that if Ollie wasn't going to read something decent, my example could at least show him that some people did, in fact, enjoy actual books. "So unhealthy," I repeated.

"*So unhealthy*," he mimicked. "*It objectifies the female blah-blah, desensitizes blah.* Shut up, dickweed. I'm thirteen and I've already kissed more girls than you have." He threw a handful of potato chips at me for emphasis, but they all came up shy.

"If you'd ever read, Oliver, you'd see. You may think I'm making it up, but studies show that men who look at too much pornography have real problems in future relationships."

In response, he held up the centerfold to me and stuck his tongue out.

"Juvenile," I said. "You can't argue facts so you try to offend."

"Spoken like a sophomore that's still not getting any," he said.

I've taught Ollie to be a skeptic, too, but he's only absorbed half the lesson; he thoroughly believes that everything he encounters, every bit of wisdom from whatever source, is entirely bogus. And for him, this sense of doubt is so universal that he refuses to put anything to the test of reason. For him, quite simply, any time somebody puts forth a claim they are "talking bullshit," and since everything is equally bullshit, there is no differentiating between one person's beliefs and another's. In that sense, refusing to believe anything people tell you is a lot like believing everything people tell you. I try to explain this to him, but, of course, he thinks I'm *talking bullshit*, so it's no use.

We simmered for a while, neither of us talking, the only sounds the canned laughter from a moronic sitcom. There was

215

a squawking outside, though, and when I pulled back the curtain, I could see, through the streaked and dirty window, two birds out by our mailbox circling fast around each other, a flurry of wings. One collided with our mailbox hard enough that it shifted on its pole, wobbling like it might topple over. They went on like that for a few minutes, darting all over our lawn, until they disappeared into the park.

"So I met the Bird Whisperer today," I said.

"Really? That guy you told me about from the news? What's his scam?"

"He swears he's on the level, but he seemed pretty weird to me."

"A guy who makes birds leave cities, gets paid for it, but just wanders off into the woods and won't let anyone know his trick? 'Weird' ain't the word. Some bullshit, if you ask me."

The next day, I got into it with Mr. Mueller, our history teacher, who seems baffled by any complex correlation between events. All he wants us to know is what happened and when, a basic chronology, names, and numbers so we can pass a standardized test and he can imagine he's a brilliant shaper of minds.

He was busy giving us the basics on World War II, using the term "Greatest Generation" so often he probably cribbed his lecture from a History Channel special. Finally, Sandra Bowman, an honor student who makes it a daily point to show us that she's studied, raised her hand to ask how the contribution by black soldiers abroad affected their struggle for civil rights at home.

Mueller paused, chalk in hands, struck dumb as a bullet. Everyone was quiet for a few seconds; even the jocks in the back row leaned forward out of their stupor, chairs creaking under their weight. I could hear a bird cheeping outside, so high and feeble that it must have been a baby. Mueller dabbed at his mustache, chalk caking the edge of his whiskers. Then he sighed and said, "Sandra, we'll talk about civil rights later in the semester. Right now, we're talking about something entirely different."

"You're joking, right?" I asked. I had buried my head into my arm, but spoke loud enough for Mueller to hear. While I suppose I should have known better, I also knew that high school is one god-awful place to be if you're content to just follow the rules.

"What was that, Benjamin?" *Benjamin* — he used my full name like it might intimidate me with formality, but names are just names, nothing magical about them.

"Do you really think that civil rights is only a discussion for after World War Two? God, you're a history teacher and you want us to think the only important things that happened to black people were the Civil War and the 'I Have a Dream' speech."

I don't even know what got into me, but I'd just read a book on the Congress of Racial Equality, and I started rattling that thing off like I was reciting the Pledge of Allegiance. But I didn't get far. "Enough," was all Mr. Mueller said, and he pointed to the door — my old marching orders to the principal's office.

When I got there, Mrs. Mahoney just shook her head. This semester we've grown to be pretty frank with each other, and instead of scolding me she usually just offers me sips of her coffee and shows me her photographs from all around the world. If I've embarrassed the right teacher — Mrs. Joseph or Mr.

Ramsey — it's all she can do not to crack a smile. She'd never admit it, but I think she wants me to make it so hard on some of them that they'll quit.

This time, though, she was not amused.

"Benny, this can't go on," she said. She showed me a picture she'd taken from her trip to Italy, asked me what I could tell her about the buildings.

"Byzantine?" I said, and she slapped the photo facedown on her desk.

"See, Ben, this is what I mean. You know how many high schoolers even know the meaning of that word?"

"I like to read," I said. "It's my thing."

"But Benny, you use your knowledge like a weapon." She sighed, but she smiled and shook her head. She has soft white hair that she's kept long when most women her age would have chopped it, and there's a natural color in her cheeks, making it impossible for her to look truly angry. "I have to do something. I'm suspending you this time."

I leaned forward so close I could smell the coffee on her desk, tried taking a serious tone like we were actually having a frank discussion about someone else: "Mrs. Mahoney, do you really think that's the best decision? Just yesterday my younger brother was looking at pornography that belonged to my father. There's very little parental guidance there."

She laughed off my efforts, not because what I said was funny, but because she was amused that I thought I could argue her down. She may be old, but she's sharp, and I like her, regardless of her status as a principal. "Ben, I know things are tough at home, but I can't control that. What I have to control is this school, so I'm telling you to go home for the rest of today, plus all of tomorrow and Friday. I can't keep giving you breaks just because I like you."

I sat outside on the steps for a while, trying to decide where to go. I told Mrs. Mahoney I'd call my dad to pick me up, but he hasn't picked me up from school in years, no matter the reason. I decided to loop through downtown, knowing I'd end up at the park but wanting to make a long trek of it. On the sidewalk, there was a dead bird, one that must have flown into the high glass wall of the gymnasium, mistaking the reflection for more sky. Ants circled it, claiming it for their own.

When I got to the park later that afternoon, there was a stack of magazines about knee-high in my hideout, a note attached from Ollie: *Bro, you like to read. These have pictures, too. Don't be afraid.*

I was busy considering how to dispose of them when I heard a rough and painful sound repeated over and over, like an animal with a bone stuck in its throat. When I looked, though, it was only Rudolph, the Whisperer, on his knees in the mud. He was calling through cupped hands, a batch of limbs strung together over his back. He'd make the sound three times, then pivot on one knee to let go of a longer, lower moan.

I watched him for a few minutes and had to admit — scam or no — he was oblivious to anything but his call. I respected that. If high school has taught me anything, it's that there's no respecting people who worry about what they look like — cheerleaders checking their makeup between classes, Mr. Poole taking his specs off and feathering back his hair whenever Mrs. Joseph swishes down the hall, the jocks making sure their baseball caps are curved *just so*. All of it sickens me. But here was

219

this guy with torn sneakers on his feet and branches on his back, a splotch of mud in the shape of Greece on the seat of his trousers, and I had to respect someone that unaware of how he looked. It was as if he were oblivious to the entire world around him, but when I snapped a twig, he stopped his call and gave a low *shhhhhhh* without ever looking at me.

He spoke in an even voice: "It's very important not to disturb them now. The finches are in a state of consideration. Give me five quiet minutes and I'll be with you, Ben."

There was not so much as a shudder in his stance for a while, and the only sounds in the entire park were his clucking and the wind ruffling the corners of my brother's magazines. Finally, the Whisperer set his leaf cover down gingerly and brushed himself off in quiet, even strokes. He walked to me, smiling as if we were meeting for lunch at a downtown diner, both of us in suits and ties. When he got close, he paused. The evening was already getting dim, most people home for dinner with their families, and he squinted in the poor light.

"What's wrong?" he asked. "What happened to you?"

I looked at myself, wondering if I'd been unknowingly injured. And though I knew the only thing bruised about me was my pride from being booted from school, being around the Whisperer made me believe in things that might not necessarily be so, and I began to imagine that I'd been cut by an avenging swordsman, shot with an arrow, blighted by some invisible curse.

"Not that," he said. "You just look like something's wrong. Anything happen to you?"

"Nothing," I said, but he kept squinting, waiting me out. "I got kicked out of school."

"You? The boy who reads the newspaper? What happened?"

"I have a bad habit of popping off at the teachers. And the principal. And, well, just about everybody else."

He scratched at his beard and looked down, almost like he was disappointed in me, and for some reason it made me feel defensive.

"It's like the teachers resent me for being smart. It's the kind of anti-intellectualism that got people killed under Stalin."

He coughed a couple times before he composed himself and told me he doubted my school operated under the same ethics as Communist Russia. He stepped closer to me, his eyes focused like he could see everything about my entire life by just this one look. Then I realized his gaze was just over my head. I looked up, but there was nothing. Just branches and leaves and sky, the same branches and leaves and sky that had always been there, the same that would be there long after old Rudolph Whitaker and I were gone.

"Let me guess," he said. He shook a couple seeds onto the ground, squinted at their pattern, then back at the spot over my head. "Are there problems at home? That's how it usually starts, acting out like this, trying to exert some type of control over your world. What about your parents?"

"Ease off there, big guy," I said. "Stick to reading the birds' minds, not mine."

He sniffed the air, decided to change the subject. "The mating habits here have been bizarre." As he said this, he shuffled a couple feet closer to me, hunched back down, and pressed a seed into the ground.

"Enough," I said.

"What?"

"This act. I mean, nobody's here to see it but me, and you already know I'm not into your whole Bird Whisperer crap." I turned away from him and squatted on a cinder block. I picked up an old paperback, its cover damp because I'd forgotten to wrap the books tight the night before. I smelled the old binding glue mix with the smell of wet earth.

"That's why I hate having people follow me when I do my work. Birds sense doubt, especially the winter wrens — and they're kind of little gossip hounds to the other birds. They're New World and Old World, you know, the winter wrens."

"Stop it. If they can smell doubt, then how come they don't smell it on me?"

He finally looked down at me, a wry grin on his face. He'd tricked me into asking that question. "Because, Benny, you don't really doubt. You're like the churchgoer who isn't entirely sure about the sermon, only in reverse — you *want* to doubt, but you don't *really* doubt yet."

"Whatever," I said, but I sounded like Ollie, petulant just for the sake of being disagreeable.

"Follow me," the man said, but he didn't go anywhere. I realized he was waiting for me to get up, but instead I leisurely finished the page I was on, hoping he'd get the hint that I didn't want to have anything to do with him. I listened to the wheeze of traffic from the nearest street, cars creeping by, people who were out and about in the middle of the week, not a goddamn care in the world. Whitaker never moved, though, and I realized that getting him to leave me alone would be like trying to get a dog to shoo once you've fed him from the dinner table.

He led me down a slight ravine near the back of the park, where Ollie and I used to play, always finding snakeskins. It looked different now, puny and cold. We stopped about half-way down by a soggy old tree stump, where he pointed to some bird droppings. He explained that he read the pattern they fell in the way other animals read one another through scent, and that there had been distress in the flocks, but they weren't ready to move just yet. All he had to do, he said, was convince them there was safety to the south, where the roads dip and twist into sprawling hills, only farmhouses dotting the landscape, too few people to be bothered.

"Yeah," I said, "and how are you gonna tell them that? Draw fake little bird prints marching south? Or maybe just play a good old-fashioned song like the Pied Piper?"

He sighed, and I knew I'd truly hurt him. It's one thing to smack down some teacher who acts like he knows everything, who's there every day like a foreman, telling you *do* or *don't*. In my book, any kind of boss deserves to catch hell whenever possible. But old Bird Man was hurt, and maybe he didn't deserve it, even if he was trying to put one over on the town.

"Sorry," I said, and I couldn't remember the last time that word came out of my mouth.

"I thought you were different," he said. "There was something about you." He nodded his head, that forlorn look of someone who should've known better, the same look my dad's had for the past two and a half years. "Inquisitive. I thought you were inquisitive."

"Fine," I said. "Tell me."

"No. Not unless you're ready to listen."

"You get my gift?" Ollie asked when I got home. I could see him in twenty years: unemployed, couch squatting, his hosts wondering how to get him away from the television and out of their house.

"Oliver, you've got to grow up."

"My teachers already say I'm a handful," he said. "How grown you want me to get?"

"It's not a compliment when they say that, Oliver."

He took a drink from a soda, his eyes on me, then threw the remote at me with his free hand. It missed and smacked against the kitchen linoleum, batteries rolling all to hell across the floor.

"You never get my point," he said. "To *me*, it *is* a compliment. Duh."

I explained that it was probably not his fault, that our culture perpetuates youth more with every generation. Long ago, we'd both be part of the labor force already, sweating the delinquency right out of us. Instead, we're given endless youth, even into our twenties and thirties, so much so that even our parents are children, and, ultimately, we're a nation of adolescents.

He responded to all this with a deliberate "Like I said. To me, that's a good thing. *Duuuh*. How can someone who reads so many books be so stupid?"

I picked up the remote, put the batteries back in, and clicked off the television. "It's a terror," I said. I pointed to the tube, and in an overly dramatic voice said, "Mind terrorist!"

This got Ollie laughing, and I remembered that when I don't take myself so seriously, he's an okay guy to be with. He grabbed the remote and turned the television back on, but just as a comfort blanket of background noise.

"I talked to that bird guy again today," I said.

"You get him to 'fess up that he's all bullshit?"

"Nah. But, you know, he honestly believes he's for real." I tried to stretch my legs out on the couch, but Ollie threw them back at me; three years younger but already stronger. "And, so, I suppose if you *believe* you're being honest, then it's a different kind of lie."

"Yeah? Maybe I can use that one next time I get caught lying in school."

Outside a bird was whooping repeatedly, and I wondered what kind it was, what kind of call. For all I'd read, spending time with the Bird Whisperer made me realize that I knew next to nothing about my natural world. Literature, history, politics, art? You got it. But ask me the difference between a poplar and a sycamore — let alone anything about birds — and I was clueless.

"You'd be proud of me, Ollie. I got booted from school today."

He raised his eyebrows in delight and smacked me on the shoulders in congratulations, like I just knocked home a winning run for our team. "Way to go, big brother. I knew you had it in you." He smiled and then shook his head, perhaps imagining how someone who might as well have a book growing from his nose could get kicked out of school. "Wish I could get booted." He rolled his eyes in frustration, then took a drink and set the can back on the carpet, dirty with paper scraps and crumbs. "Hell, the only reason to go is to try and look down Ms.

225

Morgan's top. But, man, I hate it when guys try to act like she likes them or something. I swear I was about to kick one guy's ass today."

Ollie's right about one thing: When he does grow up, he will be too much for this town to handle. If teachers think I'm a pain, they should just wait a few years, because Ollie's coming up with my lip and his testosterone — a deadly combination. When he mouths off, he might not have facts on his side, but he'll have fists. In a normal family, there would be adults cultivating what we have, feeding my reading habits, steering Oliver's energies into a more productive direction, *any* direction. Instead, we have a vacant house, the carpet unvacuumed for about a month, the television forever droning, the refrigerator with a jar of mustard and some slices of turkey long since turned.

"Where's Dad?" I asked.

Oliver shrugged his shoulders and yawned. "Better question is, where's Mom?" he said. He picked at a tear in his jeans and then sighed.

"I guess we should have been asking that question years ago," I said. "Too late now."

"Bullshit," he said. "It wasn't our job to make sure she wasn't sleeping all around town. It was Dad's job."

"I've told you, Oliver, you've got to think about that stuff rationally. It's impossible to expect every marriage to meet the ideal, and the reason Dad can't put things back together with Mom is the same reason you're so upset —" Ollie stood and shook his head, trying to interrupt me and telling me to shut up, but I wanted him to hear what I had to say. "The reason you're upset is simple male pride. But we've got to move beyond that. We've evolved, haven't we?"

226

He shouted at me, an inarticulate growl, and then punched the cushion beside my ear, a threat of the real thing. He kicked his soda can so it flipped in an arc across the living room, spinning out soda. I heard the spatter on the floor, the crazy collision of the can against our sliding glass door. Outside the bird that had been singing took off in a rush.

"Screw you, Ben," he said. "Don't sit there and defend either of them with some crap out of your books. I know what's what."

He stomped off, a small pool of soda still fizzing in the corner, and the truth is I can't say I blame him for being angry, because no matter how high I build my wall of detachment, our mother's list of infidelities is written on every brick. I went upstairs, pulled a book from the pile on my floor. I tried to read, but every time I closed my eyes all I could see were the people I'd upset that day — Mrs. Mahoney shaking her head in disappointment, Whitaker scolding me, and my brother's face red with anger.

That night, I woke up to a noise at my window. For a second, I imagined my life like another teenager's, me creeping to the window over dirty clothes and broken guitar strings instead of dog-eared books and notes, looking down to find a breathless sweetheart on the wet grass, or at least a few friends looking to make some healthy trouble. Instead, it was a bird beating its wing against my screen.

I cracked the window open, trying to be quiet. The bird was small and colored a blue so deep it looked almost black in the night, with white spots near its neck and beneath its wings. At first I thought it had somehow managed to get its wing stuck in

227

between the screen and the sill, but I realized it was merely sitting there, fluttering occasionally. I rattled the screen, hoping it would lift into the night, but it only darted its eyes in my direction. Then it sang, the sound starting deep in its throat and jumping half-octaves every beat, until it was shrill and echoing off our neighbor's house. Finally, it took off, only to swoop low across the street, zipping through the beam of an oncoming truck, then circling right back to my windowsill, chest puffed out like a band headliner.

I grabbed a shirt and a pair of jeans from my dresser. I ran outside, still barefoot, the grass wet and strewn with twigs that dug at my feet as I walked toward my window. "Get the hell out of here," I whispered, but the bird just hopped along the sill, and sang a few more notes. I looked around to see if my father had woken up, but our driveway was empty, which made two nights that week Dad hadn't made it home.

The light clicked on in Ollie's room, though, so I pinned myself up against the wall where he couldn't see me. A dirty pickup rumbled down the street, rattling as it went, and I worried about a late-night drunk hurling insults or beer cans at me. It passed by, though, and the night was quiet, chilly, and damp. Finally, I cupped my hands toward the bird, trying to be gentle, and, I swear, it hopped right in, its claws tickling the pads of my hand. It held tight, gripped on my finger as snug as a ring.

It fluttered briefly toward the road, but returned, this time latching onto my thumb as if to pull me along. Three times it repeated this, and each time I tried to rationalize what was happening: The bird had a disease, an injured wing, or was an expertly trained bird loosed on me as a practical joke, anything but what it seemed — the bird wanted me to follow. It kept

228

pulling, though, a different finger each time, and at last, against all reason, against all logical explanations, I decided, like the lemming led from a cliff, to trail right along after it.

I glanced back, but my brother's light had gone out, and all down the street there was deathly stillness, the streetlights rimmed in a mist, the only other light a soft glow from a distant living room, the television still flickering like a far-off beacon. Wet shale scraped my feet as we crossed the street, and I checked for bits of glass as I climbed over the guard rail and descended the slope toward the park. This was the opposite side of the ravine that Whitaker had led me to earlier, and as we entered the woods, I lost sight of the bird. I figured that was it; I'd seen it back to Fleming Park, and now it could dissolve back into the night, flitter and sing among the branches to its heart's content.

I don't know if it sang or not, because as soon as I lost sight of it in the mesh of limbs, a symphony of birds struck up their songs. As I edged down the slope, slipping in my bare feet, I heard them grow in power until, when I was at the bottom of the ravine, it was deafening. I was sure nobody within a mile of the park, perhaps the city limits, could sleep. It sounded like a tornado siren, only it didn't undulate, locked instead at that high whine of danger. I imagined people in town waking to its noise, scrambling to crawl spaces, the religious convinced of the Rapture, Mr. Poole rising with his face doughy white in the moonlight, eyes frightened of a real revolution, or Mr. Mueller hearing history crashing down on him at last.

I stared up in wonder as a throng of birds darkened the night sky, so many that it began to lose definition, and the whole of it was like another sky all to itself, or a churning black hole.

"Something else, isn't it?" It was, of course, Rudolph

229

Whitaker, Mr. Bird Whisperer himself. He stood on a decaying log at the bottom of the ravine, looking skyward, arms slightly raised, but not high enough to make him look like a madman or a prophet — really, he just looked like a guy mesmerized by what was happening.

"It's beautiful," I said. *Beautiful* — something not often said where I live. Our town is one of strip malls and broken streetlights, pawn shops and tobacco stores sprouting up where boutiques and bakeries used to be, everything as customized as the next town. Our courthouse limestone stained green, our war monument in disrepair, our bridges and trestles turf for graffiti wars by wannabe gangs. But this spectacle — this belonged to some other world.

"They're getting ready to go," he said. He was dressed normally, a flannel and jeans, his leather coat folded neatly across a suitcase on the ground; he could have been a man waiting for a train. "They won't be a problem here anymore."

"How did you do it?" I had to yell just to be heard over the birds.

"I talk to them," he said, patient but determined. "I really do."

"It can't be."

"Fine. You don't have to believe me, but look at them." He pointed again to the sky, where even more birds had gathered, the black hole pulsing now, as if something was about to burst forth. "And if you won't talk to me," he added, "maybe you should talk to your brother."

I turned around to see Ollie making his way down the hill, stumbling now and then and rubbing his eyes out of fatigue and disbelief. I started to tell him to go home, but the Whisperer

230

stopped me, said that Ollie should be allowed to witness this, too. Before Oliver made it all the way to us, the Whisperer sidled up to me and spoke in an easy voice: "He's always following you, you know. He's always in this park either just before you come or just after you leave, like he's tracking you." He put his hand on my shoulder, the first time I'd allowed him close enough to make contact. "He needs someone to guide him, Benny. I don't know what's happening to him, but he needs someone even more than you do."

"What's that supposed to mean?" I asked, my old strident tone rising. A brief history of child labor laws formulated in my mind, but I didn't say a word; I knew it was nothing more than a red herring, that I was afraid to confront anything, especially my brother, head-on. Instead I asked, "How would I know what to tell him?"

"How do I know what to tell *them*?" he said, pointing to the birds. "You'll get the sense of it after a while."

Ollie limped toward us, favoring one ankle that he must have twisted on his way. He wore long underwear and an oversize T-shirt he'd stolen from our dad's closet, and for all his bravado and young strength, he looked meek, his eyes blinking in the wind. He nodded at the Bird Whisperer — confirmation that all the time I'd been telling my brother about this visitor, he'd been talking to him, too.

"Dad's not home again," Oliver said, as if that were the biggest news on this night.

"I know," I said. I searched for something to say, some lesson that might make sense of our lives — our mother who'd been gone long before she moved out, our father who seems glassy and vacant even when he is there, numbing himself ounce by ounce with the liquor he keeps in the top cupboard. There was nothing, though, all of my history failing me, not a thing to tell my brother as he waited, his hair whipping around his eyes.

"Sha sha *sha!*" Whitaker shouted, his eyes glinting, calling one last order to the birds. Then he licked the edges of the mustache as he watched the sky. The birds paused in their circling and the black hole stilled, solidifying for just an instant before they took off, streaking across the sky in unison, one long, uninterrupted stretch of black. There must have been thousands, tens of thousands, the sky roiling like a tumultuous sea, all of them letting go of one last shriek as a farewell to Fleming Park, to our town.

"Nobody else will ever believe us," I told Ollie.

"I know," he said. Then he grabbed hold of me, his fingers cold and wet on my elbow. "But who cares about that?"

# ABOUT THE AUTHORS

**Coe Booth** is the author of the PUSH novel *Tyrell* and the forthcoming *Kendra*.

**Kevin Brooks** is the author of the PUSH novels *Martyn Pig, Lucas, Kissing the Rain, Candy*, and *The Road of the Dead*, as well as the forthcoming *Being*.

**Eireann Corrigan** is the author of the PUSH poetry memoir *You Remind Me of You*, the PUSH novel *Splintering*, and the forthcoming *Ordinary Ghosts*.

**Eddie de Oliveira** is the author of the PUSH novels *Lucky* and *Johnny Hazzard*.

**Tanuja Desai Hidier** is the author of the PUSH novel *Born Confused*.

**Brian James** is the author of the PUSH novels *Pure Sunshine, Perfect World, Dirty Liar*, and *Tomorrow, Maybe*, as well as the forthcoming *Thief*.

**Kristen Kemp** is the author of the PUSH novels *I Will Survive* and *The Dating Diaries*, as well as the forthcoming *Breakfast at Bloomingdale's*.

**Christopher Krovatin** is the author of the PUSH novel *Heavy Metal & You*, as well as the forthcoming *Venom*.

**Patricia McCormick** is the author of the PUSH novel *Cut*, as well as the novels *My Brother's Keeper and Sold*.

**Billy Merrell** is the author of the PUSH poetry memoir *Talking in the Dark* and is the co-editor (with David Levithan) of the anthology *The Full Spectrum*.

**Matthue Roth** is the author of the PUSH novel *Never Mind the Goldbergs*, as well as the memoir *Yom Kippur A-Go-Go*.

**Samantha Schutz** is the author of the PUSH poetry memoir *I Don't Want to Be Crazy*.

**Kevin Waltman** is the author of the PUSH novels *Nowhere Fast* and *Learning the Game*.

**Chris Wooding** is the author of the PUSH novels *Kerosene and Crashing*, as well as the Broken Sky series and the novels *The Haunting of Alaizabel Cray*, *Poison*, and *Storm Thief*.

**Markus Zusak** is the author of the PUSH novels *Fighting Ruben Wolfe* and *Getting the Girl*, as well as the novels *I Am the Messenger* and *The Book Thief*.

For more about all of these authors
check out
www.thisispush.com